OLD is a

4-LETTER WORD

By

Ethel Stockton

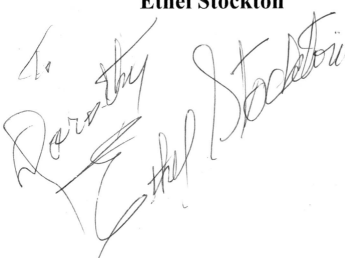

This book is a work of fiction. Places, events, and situations in this story are purely fictional. Any resemblance to actual persons, living or dead, is coincidental.

ISBN: 1-4107-9469-5 (e-book)
ISBN: 1-4107-9468-7 (Paperback)

This book is printed on acid free paper.

1stBooks - rev. 10/20/03

Dedication:

This book is dedicated to those who, regardless of their age, are willing to take a chance on life and really live it.

1

Annaliz woke up, her cheek pressed against a cold floor. Her hands slipped on the slick tile; she could not get up. Where was she?

Her rings scratched the tile as she clawed her way across the room, trying to find something to hang on to.

Pulling down her shirtsleeves, she began shoving herself along by her elbows, wincing at every movement. There at last was a chair, her favorite, the one she had repaired a month ago. Now she knew where she was, her own bedroom.

Her gnarled fingers grasped a chair leg. Trying to get up into the chair meant she had to get on her knees first and that would hurt. Why were knees ever invented, she asked herself? They always seem to be in the way. Thank God this chair is made of wood and leather and is sturdy enough to allow me to pull myself up.

Sitting on the floor, leaning against the chair to rest for a moment, she smiled, in spite of her pain, remembering when she bought the dear old thing. It was at an estate sale in Mazatlan.

Everyone told me not to buy this chair. They said it was ancient and I answered, you mean like me? It was an antique, and since I have always had a special feeling for antiques, I bought it anyway.

Karen said it was a piece of junk and should be thrown out but I knew it could be a thing of beauty if I once had a chance to do it over.

I had the gardener sand the wood and stain it an oak color. Then I rubbed the leather on the seat and back with saddle soap to make it pliable and every day I'd rub it a little more. Now it is as soft as a glove.

She caressed the leather, feeling the warmth, then took a deep breath. I'm sure glad it's here. If I can pull myself up I can sit for a minute. I don't think I have any broken bones.

What I don't need right now is a stay in the hospital. That would sure bring Karen on the run and I don't want her here. When she comes, I find myself feeling my age. I begin to think I will soon be old, which means being ill, disabled, unable to handle my own affairs, and being rushed into a rest home where I'll be forgotten.

I can't call for help. If Ed or Henry find me they'll say it's time. I can hear them now. "The old lady's done it this time. Can't get up without help when she falls? She can't stay by herself anymore."

God knows, I don't hate my sons-in-law, but I wish they wouldn't come to Mexico. I wouldn't admit it to them, but they upset me. It seems they always show up when I have other plans.

3

My daughters are bad enough. At least they stay around and take me out to dinner. The boys spend their days playing golf and ordering pizza, the food I wish had never been invented.

She got on her knees, got a solid grip on the chair's arms and slowly pulled herself up to sit in the seat, panting a little from the effort. She tried to slow her heartbeat by taking deep breaths and counting to ten but could still feel it racing.

Damn. Why did I fall? I either blacked out or I stumbled over my own feet. She looked at her hands, tanned by the many years she had lived in the Mexican sun, and wondered if she had injured them or her elbows when she was crawling. I need a manicure.

Now, why would I think of fingernails at a time like this? She looked at her hands again. Lord knows I have to have manicures to make these hands look like anything.

It's amazing what a change can be seen in just a few years. I used to have pretty hands but not any more. The wrinkles on my face tell my age but so do these thin, bony fingers.

Why do I have problems every time my sons-in-law come to visit? Maybe it's because, when the men are here, I don't get things done the way I should. I can't concentrate when they're about. I let things go until they've gone.

The boys keep telling me I'm 77 and must slow down. But, dammit, I don't want to. I plan to keep going as long as life is fun. But scares like this, make me wonder if the fun times are just about over.

My daughter's husbands have never been my favorite people. Of course, they're not crazy about me either. I hate to look at Edgar. His belly hangs so far over his belt, it's a wonder his pants stay up. Henry is not fat but thinks of himself as a dashing Romeo, which is almost as hard to deal with. He is forever looking at himself in the mirror, combing his hair or checking his teeth.

Grasping the arms of the chair with both hands, she pulled herself erect and felt her body to be sure all the parts were still there. Damn. There are times when I wish I wasn't five foot seven. It surely would be easier to pull myself up if I were only five two.

Feeling faint she limped to the bathroom, washed her face and straightened her clothes. Then, to show the world she was still around, she put on some bright red lipstick and combed her bangs.

Karen never liked my bangs. The last time she was here she said, "That's too young a fashion for you to wear, Mom. You're too old for bangs."

I said, "Well, what you say may be true but I've always liked bangs and fashion doesn't matter to me. I'll wear them if I want to. They hide my high forehead."

She left the bathroom. Edgar and Henry slouched in her living room, drinking beer. The New York Times Sunday paper was strewn around, creating a mess she hated. If there was one thing she prided herself on, it was her tidiness.

When I'm alone I know where everything is in the house. When the boys have been here a week I can't find anything.

Edgar ordered the paper when he came to Mazatlan, paying a lot of money to have it delivered. Annaliz didn't much care about the news of the world. She felt she had her own happy little world, in this house she remodeled and moved into, two years ago.

Guess I'm a loner. I really do like my solitude. Of course I love my children. But they come to see me more to watch every move I make, to reassure themselves I can still be on my own, than to be company for me. That gets tiresome.

The men had the TV they'd rented for their stay tuned to a golf tournament. Ed looked up and yelled over the announcer's voice. "Hey, Gramma. Are you okay? I thought I heard something fall in there."

"Don't know what it could have been."

No way was she going to let them know she fell. If they heard a noise why didn't they come investigate? I could have been lying there dying and they wouldn't care. Whoa, girl. Thinking such a thing is against the rules. No pity parties for you.

"We've ordered pizza," Henry said, and dropped another sheet of newspaper to the floor. "It's made with new Millennium cheese. Want to try it?"

"No. Thanks. I'll make myself something."

She planned to have a fried egg sandwich, her favorite lunch when she was alone, and a cup of coffee. How the men hated her coffee. Strong as sin it was; made from Mexican-grown coffee beans, ground just right. The boys didn't cotton too much to anything foreign.

Let's face it. They think, 'If it ain't American it ain't no good.' Well, it's their loss. I love this place, especially because it is different. I was right to decide many years ago to make Mazatlan my home.

I remember the first time I got here and went looking for a cheap place to stay. I found the La Siesta, right on the bay, a little three-story building with a patio restaurant, where a band played every noon.

It cost me ten dollars a day My room was small, just a twin bed and a chest, on the back- side of the hotel and quiet most of the time. Across the street was the beautiful blue Pacific Ocean. I loved to sit on the sea wall in the evenings and watch the sunsets. It was heaven.

The hotel gave me the first solitude I'd had in months. It was good to get away to a space of my own. I was 43 and divorced. In 1965 divorce wasn't condoned in my family. I was an outcast. I overheard people say, "Be kind to her, she must have been really desperate."

Well, I was desperate and needed to put the past behind me. I needed to go somewhere where no one knew me-where no one whispered behind my back. I wanted to start a totally new life in the sunshine.

From the La Siesta I could walk to the center of town, go to the beach or to the market, where I could enjoy all the sights and sounds of the local people selling their wares.

Pouring herself a second cup of coffee, Annaliz walked out into the sunshine, remembering: I knew I couldn't live in a hotel forever. I needed to find a place if I was going to stay. I had little money, so asked to see run-down properties.

At the first one shown me, I almost turned away, thinking it couldn't be fixed up, but when I noticed an orange tree in the back yard, in full bloom, I said, "I'll take it."

"The beams have all fallen down," the salesman, Pancho, warned.

"I can fix it." I wasn't really sure I could but I had always wanted a back yard with a tree in bloom. I felt this had to be the place God had sent me.

When I was married, I worked for a company that built spec homes. I would go out to the sites to bring papers or tools to the men. I watched them work and had some idea of how things should be done.

Why did I ever sell my first house? I was offered too much money for it, I suppose, and the challenge of doing another one appealed to me. I was into challenges in those days. I did nine houses, one right after another. It usually took me two or three years to get one finished. I enjoyed creating something out of nothing and it gave me a good income.

I wish now I had the energy to do another but I know my limitations and I think I'll stay put the rest of my life.

Annaliz took her coffee to the patio, her haven when she wanted peace. That real estate salesman, Pancho, became my first friend. His name was really Francisco, but because this was the first name of Pancho Villa, all boys named Francisco were nicknamed Pancho, after the bandit.

My friend was short, like many Mexican men, with sparkling eyes and a hearty laugh, making life fun. He hugged me every time we met and took me to all parts of the city, until I knew my way around.

We would drive to the top of Icebox hill, early in the morning, to watch the sun come up. What fun we had. She giggled. Oh, those nights...

"Hey, Granny," Henry called from the living room.

She went to the door. "Yes?"

"What are we having for supper?"

She gave him a cool, deliberate stare. "I don't know what you're having, but I think I'll have a filet mignon with a fresh green salad."

Henry frowned. "If you're having it, how come we're not having it?"

"Because I'm going to dinner with my boy friend and I don't think you're invited."

"You're kidding, of course."

"Why would I be kidding?" She smiled inside, knowing Henry and Edgar were probably taking a second look at her.

"But Grandma," Edgar blurted out, "Women your age don't have boyfriends."

She laughed out loud. "What do you know about women my age? We do all sorts of things you don't think we can do." She grinned a lopsided grin, knowing they would take her words the wrong way.

"What will Karen think?" Edgar didn't want the responsibility for this new facet of Grandma.

"Don't be stupid," Henry said. "She's pulling our leg. She doesn't mean it."

"Well, come to dinner tonight with granny and her friend and find out."

"Uh, I don't know. We better eat soon. We have a late tee-off time. We might not be back until after eight." Henry was backing down.

She could have told them Americans were the only ones who went to dinner before eight in Mazatlan. The locals usually had lunch between one and three and weren't ready for dinner until eight or after.

She really didn't want the men with her that evening. John was just back from a couple of months in the States and this would be their first chance to be together in quite a while.

His last book had been a bestseller and his commitment to his publisher meant he was gone a lot, for lectures and talk shows but, if it sold books, then he must continue.

She smiled. He loves the limelight anyway, as most of us do and, although I don't see him as much as I'd like, I'm happy for him.

Edgar and Henry are such snobs. I suppose they have so much money they think they can look down on anyone. I know they go around Mazatlan with their noses in the air. If they ask for my friend's name I'll say it is Juan instead of John. How they will hate the idea.

Henry said, "We're going to call home tonight. Do you have anything you want me to tell the family?"

She shook her head. Just like Henry. As if I can't even make my own phone calls. "Tell them I have a boy friend," she murmured. "See what they think about that."

"We'll be going home tomorrow," Edgar said. "Why don't you come with us?"

"No. Thanks."

I know what they'll do when they get home. They'll tell the girls to rush right down here and stop Grandma Annaliz, from marrying some foreigner.

Going back to the patio she settled into a chair. Seeing a flash of bright green, she called out, "Hello, Iggy. How's my favorite iguana today?"

The animal's head turned in her direction and the mouth opened slightly, as though it was meant to be a smile. The iguana was almost three feet long and looked old. Even though he was still a bright green, the hairs on the top of his back were dark. He was reclining on top of the garden wall, amid the broken glass. She wondered how he could get between the pieces to be comfortable.

He began to move away slowly.

Annaliz said aloud "Don't leave. Take it easy. We're just two friends enjoying the sunshine. Stay awhile."

The iguana had found her garden when she first planted it. He loved to eat the leaves of most plants. At one time she'd had to fence him out but now he ate only a little and she didn't bother.

There were many geckos on the high walls of the patio at all times but she didn't try to keep them out either. They ate the flies and mosquitoes.

She tried to concentrate on writing a few bits of poetry, needing to have a new poem to read at the next meeting of the Poet's Corner, but couldn't think of a single line.

Being a teacher can be a problem. How can I ask my students to bring a poem to class each time if I can't write a poem every week?

I once was considered a poet. My poems were published in a book about ten years ago. I was a celebrity then. Well. Time goes by. I still write but the spark I once had seems to escape me. Now I have to work to get even the simplest sentence.

She kept thinking of what Edgar had said about being too old to have boyfriends. I know he is over 50. Has he already given up having sex? Maybe he has. He's so fat, I don't know how he finds it to pee, much less gets it up.

And Henry. He's full of Henry and there's no room for anyone else. How does Tiffany stand him? She was always the sensitive one in the family.

I know just the kind of man Tiffany needs. She smiled, remembering Jorge: He had the lightest, feathery touch... Tears began to fall and she scolded herself. Don't cry, girl. You cried enough for him when he died in the bus crash.

They said his bus was broad-sided by a double-semi running a red light. Every one on the bus was killed. I couldn't believe it, when they told me. I was devastated. We had only decided the week before, that he might as well move in with me. We had planned a vacation together in Guadalajara.

I know the family would never have approved of Jorge. He was a

Mexican bus driver and beneath them. I didn't care what work he did. He was everything to me. He was the light of my life. I miss him and shall love him forever.

When she heard the men go out to play golf, she went back in the house to tidy up. It would be easier when the girls came to see her. "At least they don't leave pizza boxes with half-eaten food in them," she muttered.

Stop it! She spoke harshly to herself. You promised you would never let yourself mutter and here you are doing it. Do you want to show your age?

I hope my daughter, Tiffany, comes this time, instead of Karen. Karen is welcome but she can be tiring. Tiffany is happy to sit in the patio and be silent for hours.

The last time Karen came she scowled and said, "You've been down here for over 30 years. It's time to come home."

Then she crossed her arms, like an old washer woman, and said loudly, "You're getting along, and soon you won't be able to take care of yourself. I'm only telling you this for your own good, Mom."

I said, "I may be getting along, but I don't want 'good.' I had what everybody else called good over 30 years ago. What I need are fun things and maybe even something a little risqué. If I can't have that now, when can I? I was told, and believed, 'things will get better when you're older.' Well, they didn't. They got worse until I went ahead and did what I knew was right for me."

Karen almost jumped out of her skin when I stomped my foot and said, "Damn it. I'm not going to ruin it now by going back where people will try to tell me what to do. I may be in my second childhood but I don't need diapers."

"Mom." Karen screamed at me. "You swore. I've never heard you swear. When did you start? Women don't swear."

"There are times, Karen, when swearing is the only thing that will express exactly how I feel. Try it some time why don't you? You need to relax."

"I may need to relax but I'm a mature woman and mature women do not swear."

I said, "My dear, you may be ripe but I don't think you're mature. Leave that to women my age."

2

As Annaliz expected, it was Karen who arrived, yelling her words of disapproval.

"Mom, it's silly to think of you with a boyfriend. At your age! What will our friends say?"

"Karen, I moved down here for that very reason. I wanted to be someone different but I didn't want to embarrass you. Now you want me to change the way I live. I won't do it."

Karen changed the subject. "But Mom. What if you fall and there is no one here to help you? I worry about you."

"That's your problem. Not mine. What if I don't fall and live another 20 years? It's silly to even think about it."

Annaliz held her body rigid so the twinge in her knee, which was still there after yesterday's fall, wouldn't show. She certainly wasn't going to tell Karen about that. She'd be ready to ship me back to a nursing home. One of the things I like best about living here is, I don't have to listen to Karen say, "You should…".

"Mom. I only think you should slow down a little."

"Now you're being silly. You know I'm never going to 'slow down' as you call it. That phrase is misused when talking of my generation. Most of us are trying to move a little faster. No," She shook her head. "You can slow down, but I was only starting to grow at 47, and I wish you would too."

She put out her hand to touch her daughter's shoulder. "Come on, honey, do something different now and then. Grow a little."

Karen drew herself up to her full five-foot-five, tossed back her mane of dark hair and said. "I am growing. I'm reaching out. I'm teaching a child to read. I'm serving on the board of a home for battered women. I am doing things."

"Yes, you are and I applaud it. But, stop and think: When was the last time you had fun? When was the last time you did something for yourself?"

"I'm doing those things for myself."

"Are you really? Or are you doing them because it's expected of you, or because your friends do them and you want to belong?"

"Mom, why do you dislike my doing those things? I'm busy and fulfilled."

"Ha!"

Karen became indignant. Her face turned red. "And just what do you mean by 'Ha!' in that tone of voice?"

"When was the last time you had sex? I don't mean going to bed with Edgar. I mean sex."

Karen screamed. "My sex life is not your business. How could you even ask that question? What kind of mother are you?

"I'm the type that can tell, from what you just said, that you meant to say - Not in a hell of a long time."

"That's a lie. We have sex all the time."

"You mean every Saturday night, rain or shine, as in 'Let's get this chore over with?' What fun is that?"

"Mom, why are you doing this to me?"

"I'm not the one, honey. You are. You have carved out a neat little rut for yourself. Then you say, 'All my friends are living the same kind of lives and they seem happy.' Don't do this, please. Learn to live a little. Contentment is for cows."

"I don't understand. I thought all one needed in life was to be content. Most people are okay with it."

"See. You are classing yourself with 'most people.' Do you want to be one of the cows in the pasture? Oh, for pity's sake, go out and have some fun. Take a look around, as I did."

"You mean run away to Mexico?"

Her mother laughed. "Yes, even Mexico, if necessary. See the world with new eyes. Meet new people."

"You mean men, I suppose. You've always got a man around you. I don't need them. What do you see in men? What do they have to offer you? I would never have an affair."

Oh, God. Annaliz groaned. I don't know if Karen brings out the worst in me or the best in me, but I need to teach her to smell the roses.

"Maybe not." she said. "but if that's what it takes, to wake you up to the wonders outside the rut you are in, then go for it."

"I can't believe this." Karen's face darkened in what her mother knew was her most disapproving frown. "How disgusting. My own mother telling me I should have an affair."

"You don't have to have an affair. Why do you misconstrue my words? You seem to think in order to get out of your rut you need a new man. There are other things you can do just as exciting."

You liar. She chuckled inwardly. The most exciting thing in the world is a new man. I remember when I met Renaldo - over six feet tall, and built like a Greek god. We hit it off immediately. There was certainly the right kind of chemistry between us…

"Mom." Karen yelled to get her attention. "Are you listening?"

"Oh, sorry. I was thinking. Why not come to dinner tonight at the Playa? My friends and I go on Friday nights to eat, drink and watch the sunset."

"I suppose you drink Mexican Tequila," Karen said scornfully.

"At times. It's not my favorite. I like vodka martinis better."

"Are you still drinking those things? You know they're not good for you. The doctor said you should drink wine instead. 'One glass of red every day.' he said. He told you to leave the martinis alone."

"I happen to like martinis better than wine."

"Mom. Why won't you do what the doctor tells you? Do you want to die?"

"Karen, I have to die sometime. I've made plans. I'd rather it happened while I'm drinking a martini, instead of with a stupid glass of red wine in my hand."

"Oh. You always make fun of what I say; you have an answer for everything. Why can't you be like other mothers?"

Karen sighed. "All right. Now, tell me about your friends I'm going to meet, if I go to this dinner. I suppose I should know something about them. Are all of them your age? Is any one of them a favorite?"

Annaliz knew Karen was searching for the name of her boyfriend, which she didn't intend to tell her yet.

She said, "Ramona has been my friend for 30 years. When we first met she was a reporter for the local paper. When I was learning Spanish she helped me a great deal." She laughed. "I remember the first time she took me shopping. I thought I knew enough Spanish to get by but, in the department store, I headed for an area with a sign that said, Recamara. She asked where I was going. I said I needed film for my camera. She informed me recamara meant bedroom, not camera." Annaliz shook her head. "Ramona said to me, 'Now, if you want a mattress you'll know just where to go,' and she laughed with me. We have been close friends since then and we often have dinner at each other's homes."

She continued, "and Maria, Estrella and Lenora will be there, with probably a few more of my pals. They all seem to show up for Friday dinners."

She sat thinking of Ramona. She was the one who introduced her brother, Gilbierto. He was shy and I found he was a very sensitive person. He knew I needed a friend, without me telling him. I needed someone to confide in, and he became that for me. When I tried to feel sorry for myself he would laugh and then I found myself laughing too. What fun it is to laugh with friends.

We never became lovers. Our friendship meant too much to each of us. He died of a heart attack in 1997. I miss him. There will never be another like him.

She finally heard Karen's voice. "Mom, you're not listening to me. I asked if you wanted to go shopping."

"No, I think not. I have things to do."

"What kind of things?" Her voice said it all. The things her mother did couldn't possibly be important.

"Well, if you must know, I have to write a poem to take to class on Tuesday night, then finish reading a book we'll be discussing on Thursday night…"

"Mom," Karen broke in. "You're driving at night? At your age?"

Annaliz knew, if she heard the phrase 'your age' one more time she would vomit, but said only, "I can take care of myself."

"But you told me about your friend who was killed coming home one night…"

"Oh, Karen, for pity's sake. Go shopping."

When Karen had gone, Annaliz reflected on the passing of her dearest friends and family. What hurt most about growing older was the loss of many people who had added so much to her life.

My siblings are gone. Elsie was like Karen, forever criticizing others, demanding they conform to her way of doing things. Danny was just the opposite. He was like I am now, laughing all the time, happy with his life and his family. I miss them both but Danny most of all. He brought joy into my life when I really needed it.

Friends from my younger years have gone. I miss Janey. We knew each other since the first grade and when she died two years ago, I didn't think I could stand it. I felt alone for a time, but I don't brood for very long. I've learned to accept whatever comes in life. I can make all the plans I want but it won't make a difference in the long run. There isn't a great deal I can do to keep sad things from happening.

I guess I'm the last leaf on the tree. Thank God I still have my kids. I have a lot of friends but they're not the same as family. We may not always think alike and sometimes we argue, but it's nice to know they're still in the world. We don't live near each other, but we do love each other. I'm really fortunate to have such a large, caring family.

Why does it make such a difference to Karen where I die? Death will come, no matter where I live. One must accept it. But she is right. I do need a keeper at times. The fall yesterday made me realize it could happen again, and I might not be able to get up next time. I'll make plans for Aurilia, my maid, to come in every other day, instead of just once a week to clean. She has a key, so if I can't manage by myself, or fall, she can take care of me.

She pushed back her white bangs and grinned. John, if asked, would say he'd like to be my keeper, but I don't want a keeper. Most of the time I want to be left to sit and enjoy the sunshine alone. I'm not anti-social. I happen to like solitude."

Relieved by her plan to have her maid take more responsibility, Annaliz went to the bedroom for a nap. Why do the family insist I have a nap every day when I'm home? It's as though I would drop dead if I didn't have one. I don't need a nap, no matter what anyone else may think, but it lets me stay up longer at night and dinner at the Playa does go on and on.

Lying there, dozing, she began thinking of how her life would be if she moved back to the States. I'd have the whole clan on my shoulders. I'd no longer be Annaliz, as I am here. I'd be Grandma. They wouldn't have to chain me down but the weather in that Northwest city would keep me housebound. I'd be expected to sit in my chair and give out advice which no one will take. They'd turn down my bed and insist I take a nap every afternoon.

I wouldn't be allowed to laugh out loud. They'd say it's not lady-like. My martini intake would be monitored or stopped altogether. If I wanted to venture out on my own, someone will be sure to say it's not a good idea. I can hear them now: "You shouldn't try to do too much at your age."

My Lord, she thought, If I go back there, I'll no longer be a human being. I'll be the Matriarch. I'll be the aged one. They'll treat me as though I'm older than Eve, and God forbid I should have any fun. I do love my kids but they can be a pain sometimes.

Once Henry, who has never really liked me, told me I was a stubborn old woman. Thank God I am. I'm staying right here.

As she drifted off to sleep, she smiled, a small child's impish smile, and added, "with Juan."

3

The usual table was set for the Friday Dinner Group at the Playa restaurant. From Annaliz' vantage point she saw the lights of the city she loved. The curving sea wall, with the glow of the tall buildings behind it, ran the full distance of the main part of Mazatlan. It was a scene she never tired of seeing. The tide was coming in and, if she listened carefully, she could hear the swish of the waves moving in and out.

She loved seeing tonight's sunset, which was especially spectacular. Brilliant reds, purples and golds streaked across the sky as though trying to outdo each other. The small islands, out in the bay, were black silhouettes against the brilliant color.

Annaliz turned to ask her daughter how she liked it. Karen wasn't looking at the sunset. She was sniffing the air as if she smelled something bad. She was not at her best when meeting new people, but surely she could take time out from thinking of herself to enjoy the beauty of the area.

She is missing so much, Annaliz thought. I don't know what I would do if I couldn't appreciate the lovely things I see every day.

I know she is used to dealing with first graders, but she must talk to their parents. How can she be so rude to Ramona, who is twice her age, and is only trying to be friendly? Karen spoke no Spanish and Ramona's English left much to be desired, yet, Annaliz knew, one can be understood, if one wants to, even with sign language.

Is Karen jealous of Ramona because she's my friend? For some reason my daughter finds fault with any one I like. Maybe she doesn't want me to have friends. She may feel if I didn't have any, I would be willing to go back home.

Perhaps I should have chosen some other way for her to meet John. I could have made other plans.

Estrella, the tallest and prettiest of Annaliz' friends, was dressed in her usual flamboyant style. She wore a huge hat, high-heeled sandals, and her dress today was made of feathers and such thin stuff it floated as she walked.

Every head turned when Estrella walked into the room. Who would have nerve enough to come to a local restaurant, looking so exotic, when everyone else was in everyday clothes? For Estrella, these were her everyday clothes. No one had ever seen her wear any other kind.

Her husband, Pedro, always followed in her footsteps, as though showing her homage and, Annaliz thought, she deserves it more than most because she is so daring. None of the other women I know would dare wear sequins and feathers in public to go to dinner. I know I might wear something like it to the theatre or opera but not to the Playa.

Karen had finally consented to attempt conversation with Lorena, who taught retarded children. She wore her hair in a bun, had glasses and dressed in a business suit. Maybe she fit Karen's image of how a teacher should look.

I should have known they would get along, Annaliz thought. I'm glad Lorena's here. Maybe Karen will relax a bit with her.

Although there was a language barrier, Lorena was about her age and Karen seemed willing to try to understand, for she wanted to talk about her work, teaching art to a first grade class in Cameron, her home town.

Maria, another friend at the table, raised her eyebrows and grinned at Annaliz, as if to say "Are we having fun yet?" Maria was the most fun-loving woman of them all. Always ready for any outing, Maria was sure to come up with some outrageous idea of where to go and what to do next. She was roly-poly, only five foot two, with a light-up-the-room kind of smile. She had a tendency to pull others to her ample chest and kiss them on both cheeks. Although this was a local custom, when Maria did it, her friends knew she meant it. Everyone loved her, accepted her practical jokes and waited for her next party.

The last of her parties was at Thanksgiving. She surprised everyone with turkey and all the trimmings. Her stuffing didn't have enough sage in it to please everyone but it was good. The mashed potatoes were made from Potato Buds, which can be purchased in Mazatlan, and the gravy tasted like poultry gravy.

How she did it was a mystery to Maria's friends. She had never prepared anything but Mexican food before.

Turkey is plentiful in Mexico so no one was surprised to see it on the menu, but Annaliz asked others at the table, "Where do you suppose she got the pumpkin pie spices? It tastes just like home." Maria finally admitted she'd had her sister, who lived in Denver, send a can of pumpkin with the spices. Everyone agreed they had eaten a meal very similar to the kind eaten in the States for the holiday.

They went to Maria's parties with enthusiasm, as she loved to cook dinners and to get together with other people. She always came to the hotel on Friday nights.

Annaliz looked around the hotel dining room, which was huge and built on the beach. It overflowed with flowers and ferns to soften the look of so many tables and chairs. She liked the way the area was lit by candles on the tables and tall torches near the water. She watched, after sunset, when the flame of the torches, moving in the breeze, gave everything a festive look.

The women cashiers were dressed in their usual black and white uniforms and the men waiters were in simple white shirts and black pants.

It always amazes me, Annaliz thought, how the waiters give their orders to the cashier and she keeps a copy until I pay. Waiters carry money only to give it to the cashier. The cashiers are always women. I wonder why.

She realized every restaurant she frequented did the same thing. It took a long time to get the cuenta, or bill.

Waiters have to run to the cashier, get the bill, bring it to me, take my credit card, run back to the cashier, get the ticket and bring it for me to sign and return to the cashier, who double checks the charge. Then I get my card back.

Oh, well, in Mazatlan, time means nothing. Anyway, most restaurants bring you a free drink of Kalua and cream while you're waiting for your change, which is lovely.

Annaliz looked at Karen. She's getting anxious. She's been twisting around in her seat when she thinks I'm not looking. I know she's watching for my boy friend. I wonder what type of person she thinks he'll be? Probably some old bald-headed guy with a cane, and one foot in the grave. I'm sure she can't imagine me having a boy friend ten years younger than I am. What a disgrace. She wouldn't want the neighbors to know about it. If I really want to get her going, all I have to do is tell her I have plans with him.

Thinking of plans made her smile. Lately it seems I am making plans for everything I do. When did I begin to get so organized? I've always been spontaneous. What is this sudden urge to know what the next day will bring?

I've heard it said the older one gets, the more organized they want to be. I'd better quit right now, but it is fun.

She looked at Karen, sitting so stiffly in her chair, and wondered if the poor girl ever relaxed. She's like a bulldog, watching every move, waiting to be told who to bite next.

I hope she's not going to ask where John is, or why he didn't come. He's usually on time. I wonder why he's late. Perhaps I was too harsh in trying to describe her to him. I only wanted to let him know she could be inconsiderate and condescending.

Could I have scared him off? I'm beginning to think he's afraid to meet her and stayed home.

As they were eating their dessert of caramel flan, there was a commotion at the entrance to the bar and John appeared. Staggering across the room he yelled, "Liz, you'll never guess what's happened."

There was a sudden silence around the table. She had told her friends how straight-laced Karen was and they knew both of them could be embarrassed by what had just happened. They were sure there would be a flare up, right at the table.

Annaliz met John halfway across the room and took his arm to lead him away. Jose, the bartender, came out and took his other arm and said, "Sorry, Senora. I didn't see him head for the dining room. He seemed to be all right in the bar. I'll take him back."

"It's not your fault, Jose. Send him home in a cab, please."

When she came back to the table Karen stood up, her brown eyes dark as coal, her wide hips solidly planted. "Let's go home," she said.

As Annaliz reached for her sweater on the back of her chair, she noticed Ramona looking at her with concern. She knows it's not going to be a fun evening. Trying to make it seem as though nothing were wrong, Annaliz dropped money on the table to pay her bill, waved to her friends, said, "See ya," and walked away.

There was silence in the car for a long time and then Karen said, "So. Your boyfriend is a lush."

"Yes. Sometimes he is."

"And he calls you Liz. You've never let anyone in the family call you Liz."

"He only does it when he's drunk." To herself she added, or when we're alone.

It's odd, but true, no one else has ever attempted to give me a nickname, maybe because I wouldn't have allowed any one else to do so. John can persuade me to do things I might not do otherwise. Most of the time I'm happy to do what he suggests.

She realized Karen was still talking.

"Mom, how can you stand him?"

"Well, most of the time he's sober. Some things begin to prey on his mind and he gets as you saw him. I know it wasn't pretty but it's not the end of the world."

"For Heaven's sake. Surely you don't want people to know you have a drunk for a boy friend."

"They all know it, my dear. It's common knowledge. My friends just ignore him when he's in his cups and I do to as much as I can. If we leave him alone he usually goes home and sleeps it off."

"Mom. Why do you put up with him? You know we don't have drunks in our family."

Annaliz said, "Come on, Karen. Where have you been all your life? What about Gilbert, your cousin?"

"He's an exception."

"What about Sidney Wales at that gorgeous country club of yours? He's a real lush if I ever saw one. You don't shun him. Is it because he has so much money?"

"Money has nothing to do with it."

"No? What if I told you John could buy and sell Sidney about four times?"

"You're kidding."

47

"No. Five years ago John wrote a best-seller, one of the biggest ever published. It was made into a movie called King's X. He's wealthy."

She turned to Karen. "You must have seen him on TV. He did all the talk shows, all the public appearances any successful author gets. He's paid well now, when he lectures, which is quite often."

"If he's so rich why does he have to drink?"

"Why does anyone drink? They want to forget their fears. Although he won't admit it, I think John's afraid to write another book. He's sure it would be a failure and he'd become a laughing stock in literary circles. He wouldn't be able to stand it. He's still being treated like a star and he doesn't want to lose that feeling."

Karen was silent as they pulled into the garage, then said, "Why do you keep seeing him, Mom?"

"I suppose it's because I've had my bad moments."

"Not drunk, I hope."

"Feeling sorry for yourself to the point of desperation is almost as bad."

"When did you ever feel desperation?" Karen's voice rose to its highest point of disagreement, as if to say, "If you felt that way why wasn't I told? You've been keeping things from me."

Annaliz said, "A friend I loved very much died and John was there at the right time, holding my hand, giving me a shoulder to cry on. I never forget those thoughtful things someone does for me."

"Then he isn't your boyfriend?"

"He's a very dear friend."

"And who was the friend that died?"

Annaliz was not going to get into a fighting match with Karen over Jorge. His memory was too sacred to share.

She said, "Just one of my friends."

"Oh." Karen wasn't interested in the past. She wanted to know about the boyfriend. "How did you meet John?"

"He bought one of the houses I remodeled. You remember the fifth one? It had such a large patio, I put in a fish-pond."

"Did you know he was a drunk then?"

"No, but I wouldn't have cared."

"Shouldn't you try to get him to stop drinking? A friend would certainly try."

"No, my dear. Down here, that is exactly what a friend would not do. In Mazatlan every one is given the opportunity to live his life exactly as he wants. No one tries to tell you what to do. They're not interested in your life style. They love you for what you can add to their lives."

She sighed. "Sometimes it's just being thankful when one can say, 'There but for the Grace of God go I.' and mean it."

Karen was silent. Shaking her head, Annaliz continued, "Tolerance by my friends, their ability to overlook other's frailties, is perhaps what keeps me here. If John wants to kill himself by drinking, it's his choice. No one will try to stop him and no one will criticize."

She took a deep breath. "I stay, because like him, I want no interference in how I live or die."

Karen gave a quick look in her direction and then looked away. No more was said that night. Karen flew home the next morning and it was never mentioned between them again.

4

John appeared in Annaliz' kitchen a few days later. No apologies were given, or needed. He helped himself to a cup of coffee and said, "I'm going to the States in December."

He took a deep drink and put the cup down, then drew himself up to his full five-foot-ten, straightened his broad shoulders, spread his arms as wide as they would go and announced in a pompous voice. "I've been invited to lecshaw at Hawvawd."

Annaliz loved to see the light in his blue eyes when he was excited. He really was a darling man, when he wasn't drunk, and she knew she would accept him as he was, for she wanted to continue to be his friend. Life was much more complete when he was around. I do hope he'll get a haircut before he goes. That white fluff of his is almost over his ears.

She said, "How wonderful, John. Harvard will truly be a feather in your cap."

"I'm not sure how to lecture to those wealthy kids. Do you think I should deviate from the book?"

"Heavens no. *King's X* is about macho men. I'm sure those boys would like to know how to be one."

He frowned. "It's been five years since I wrote it. Do you suppose they'll ask me why I haven't written another one? They'll surely ask me when the next one's coming out."

"So what? Authors don't talk about their next book. It isn't done. No one expects it."

"People have asked before. You know I get panicky when that happens. What will I do?"

"For Pete's sake, John, grow up. When are you going to stop worrying about what people think? Just get on with your life…" She stopped.

He was giving her that look that said, "Don't you dare do this to me."

He looked her over from head to toe and said, "What did I ever see in you? You're too tall and too skinny."

She laughed. "Yes. I am."

"You have wrinkles on top of wrinkles and," he paused, "and those green eyes of yours can look downright mean."

She laughed again. "John, you can't hurt my feelings by telling me things I already know."

He tried to frown. "I know a lot of women like you who prey on us younger guys. Vipers!"

Even he had to grin. He knew he was only ten years younger.

Annaliz shot back, "If you've known that many of my kind of woman, why don't you write a book about them?"

"By God, I think I will."

She knew, in the next few weeks, that John was writing again. He didn't call, didn't appear in the bars and his phone was disconnected. She didn't try to reach him, because she knew, when he was writing, he wanted no one else around.

She spent her time instructing the gardener where to plant the herbs she had decided would be a big boon to her cooking. She knew she wasn't a good cook and hoped she might do better if she used fresh herbs.

John's agent called her from New York. "I'm trying to reach John. His phone's been cut off. Is he all right?"

"I haven't talked to him but I think he's doing fine. I'm sure he's writing a new book. You know, Jeff, he doesn't want anyone around when he's doing that."

Jeff sighed. "Oh, God, if I thought he was. It's been five years. I was about to give up on his ever having another book. How did you get him to do it?"

"I take no responsibility. I think he was ready."

"Yeah. I know how you are. You must have pushed him. No one else has ever been as helpful to him as you have. He may never admit it but he leans on you."

She argued, "I've never envisioned John as a leaner."

"When he's here, in New York, you're all he talks about. He says he's living in what was once Liz's house and some people think he's talking of Elizabeth, but I know different."

He went on. "He's proud of your achievements. He thinks your poetry is outstanding. By the way, if you need a new agent let me know."

She said, "Thanks, Jeff. I'll keep it in mind. I haven't written much lately."

Jeff laughed, "You need a Liz in your life to push you. Call me, please, when John surfaces."

Why haven't I written much poetry in the last few months? This has been a good year. The vegetable garden looks great. I'll probably have enough zucchini to feed the neighborhood, and my flower garden has been such a joy.

Having fresh flowers in the house every day has always been one of my dreams and here it comes true because I can cut my own any time I want.

She had moved her special chair out to the patio and as she settled into it and heard the leather creak, she knew she was where she really wanted to be. The palm fronds from the coconut tree in the neighbor's yard swayed and rustled in the breeze and the scent of orange blossoms filled the air where she sat relaxed.

Maybe I only write when there's a special occasion. Yes, that's probably it. I remember when Caroline, Tiffany's oldest daughter, was married; I wrote a poem for her. That was a happy time.

She got married on the beach, of all things. What ideas these young people have nowadays. One of her friends was even married at a ski lodge.

I remember trying to stand still in the sand while Caroline answered the minister. I have to admit my balance is not too great and I had to lean a bit on Edgar, who was standing next to me. I couldn't help but notice that the beautiful, pale blue boots the bride wore, were getting scratched up and dirty, as she also tried to keep her balance. I bet she didn't think about that when she chose the place to get married.

Caroline and her groom wrote most of the words to say at the ceremony. That wouldn't have been allowed when I tied the knot. We were heavily into tradition in those days.

Many women marry in a church. I married at home. We didn't have much but my mother insisted on a dinner for the guests. I invited only fifteen people because I knew we couldn't seat more than that.

Most women did get married at home during the Great Depression, just before the war. No one could afford a big church wedding. I remember the minister cost the groom ten dollars, which was a lot in those times, and my wedding dress, purchased at J C Penny, cost $3.95, on sale. I liked it because of the low bodice and full skirt, and the fact it was made of white, dotted Swiss.

Poetry is not necessarily about happy times but I prefer writing poems when I'm pleased with life. I think that was why my book was a small success. I was with Jorge and life then was really happy times.

The plans I'd made, for both of us, seemed to be working out. We'd only known each other a year but that was the most wonderful year of my life.

Writing poems again, after he died, seemed senseless. I seem to be able to do it now only when necessary for my poetry class.

What I need, is another happy occasion.

5

When Tiffany called the next day to say her daughter, Morgan, was getting married, Annaliz wondered if she'd been sharing their excitement, all the way from the state of Washington.

She said, "I won't come for the planning. I don't want to be in the middle of the chaos, but I'll certainly be there for my granddaughter's wedding. Just tell me what she wants and the date. I promise I'll arrive."

Tiffany said, "It won't be for six months. Morgan thinks it will take months to get everything arranged the way she wants it. She said if she waits until your birthday you'll be sure to attend."

"But this isn't the year you celebrate my birthday, Tiffany. I'll be 78. You only do it every five years."

"I told her, but she said it would be easy to remember her anniversary if she knew it was on your day. She's planning a traditional church wedding and wants to be sure you'll come."

She went on. "The dress she's looking at has a train long enough for a movie star. It will cost a mint but Henry isn't saying a word. Of course, since it's Morgan, his baby girl, he'll spend whatever she wants."

Tiffany hesitated, "Mom, may I ask you something?"

"Of course. Anything."

"How old were you when you started writing poetry?

What a strange question. I wonder what made her ask? I didn't know anyone in the family was interested in poetry. They've never said anything about my book of poems published ten years ago. They laughed when I said, at the time it came out, "Now I'm a poet." I don't think they were impressed.

Annaliz said, "I must have been about 43 or so. It was after my divorce, when I was on my own, just before I came to Mexico. I went to a writer's class at the local college. Why? Are you thinking of taking it up?"

She could hear a sigh. "I've been writing for a long time."

"Why didn't you ever show me?"

"I was afraid you'd laugh. After all, you're a published poet. My writings would be silly alongside yours."

"Poetry comes from the heart. It doesn't matter if it's my heart or yours, dear. Your poetry may even be better than mine."

She said to herself, I'm sure yours will be fresher than mine. I've used and abused my heart so many times over the years I'm not surprised I have difficulty getting anything down on paper.

Tiffany said, "Mom, you give me such hope. I have shown my poems to

Henry and he's passed them off as not worth reading. He won't take me seriously."

What a clod! I always knew there was a reason I didn't care for her husband.

"Don't listen to him, Tiffany. Don't show your work to anyone but your teacher. Keep writing something every day, however, even if you think it might be just gobble-de-gook, as Henry might say."

She went on. "Doing the writing is the only thing that will make you a better poet but it helps to have a teacher. It means each time you go to class you have to have a new poem to show. It keeps you on your toes. When I come to the wedding we'll sit down together and talk about it, if you'd like. You always got straight A's in English as I recall. Poetry should be easy for you."

"I love doing it," Tiffany said. "But I always wonder whether or not it's good enough. I can hardly wait to talk to you. Six months can be an awfully long time. Do come soon. I love you."

Annaliz hadn't looked at her book of poetry for a long time. Now she got it out and read all afternoon. I wonder why I can't write like I used to. Perhaps it's because this book was written when I was with Jorge. He liked the things I wrote and kept insisting I get a publisher.

Once I wrote a poem about Gato, his cat. Gato is Spanish for cat and we never gave him another name.

The animal loved to sleep by the wall in a low place, almost a cave. I called the poem *Gato in the Grotto*. It was the only time I tried to write a humorous one. Jorge laughed until he cried.

He also inspired romantic ideas in my head. When I wrote of love, I was writing about him. Just to look at his dark hair, his deep brown eyes…Oh, damn, there come the tears again. I still miss him so much.

Perhaps one of the reasons I love John is because, he knows how much I loved Jorge, and he gives me space to think about him when I need to.

Somehow, the thought of Tiffany being interested in poetry, gave her an incentive to work at her own again. I don't want to do a book, just a few pages to keep my mind active. She wrote off and on, for the next few months, thinking it would be interesting to see the differences in her writing and Tiffany's.

Six months later Annaliz flew to the States a few days before the wedding. John was lecturing at the University of Washington in Seattle. She was sure he would be talking about the new book. She still didn't know everything about it. He didn't like to discuss it with her before he had the whole thing out to his editor. He'd been busy writing for the last six months and she had seen little of him.

I'll go to the lecture because I've never seen him perform. She was impressed. John had an easy way of making the audience understand what he was talking about. He even told the basic plot of the new book. Then, to her horror, he said one of his women friends had been the inspiration for it. She was relieved when he didn't give her name. She slipped away at the end of the lecture so he wouldn't know she had been there.

Arriving back again, at what she laughingly called the old homestead, she wondered why there was so much excitement at her coming home? You'd think I was the Queen of England the way people are falling over themselves to welcome me. She grinned. They must think I've come into money...

Oh, oh. I bet Karen put them up to it. She'll never give up trying to make me stay close to her and it isn't because she's so fond of me. Most of the time we're arguing. She thinks I'm in my dotage and should give up and come home where someone - I think she wants it to be her - can take care of me.

She's sure I'd be better off in one of those 'Assisted Living' facilities, where she could tell the managers just how to take care of her mother. I am never going to give in. I certainly do not want to live with a lot of old folks.

Annaliz had just settled into her recliner in the family room when her granddaughter came in. "Morgan. How wonderful to see you. How's the bride?"

"Oh, Grandma. Everything has come apart." Morgan fell sobbing into her grandmother's lap.

"Come now. This is no way to act. The wedding is tomorrow."

"No. It isn't. It's been called off. Derek is already married. His wife and child came here this morning."

It took an hour to tell her the whole story. They all liked Derek. He seemed like such a nice boy. He and Morgan had set the date. The gorgeous dress was hanging in the closet ready for the next day. The flowers had arrived at the church and the decorations were complete.

Somehow, his wife in Texas heard of the impending marriage and arrived that morning in time to stop the ceremony.

Annaliz started to say, men didn't do those kinds of things in my day, then caught herself. My day? I never use those words. It reminds me of how many days I've had.

If I'm beginning to think in those terms, I'd better hurry back to Mexico, and why in the world would I think men didn't do those kinds of things when I was young? Of course they did. I should know.

The next afternoon it was an uneasy family dinner, gathered together to talk about anything and everything, except the wedding Morgan hadn't had. Every one felt sorry for her but didn't know how to help her.

A great grandchild spoke up, "Grandma, what are you going to be when you grow up?"

There was a loud guffaw from Edgar. "Grandma is never going to grow up. Isn't that right, Granny?"

She gave him one of her well-known stares and said, "There has to be one smart-ass in the family. I guess you were picked because you fit the image so well."

Every one laughed.

Annaliz turned back to the child and said, "What an interesting question, Lionel. Why do you ask?"

"Cousin Eliot told me everyone should decide before they get too old."

She was astounded at how many times in one's life the word 'old' came up. We all seem to be delineated by how old we are.

To Lionel she said, "And have you planned what you will be?"

"I don't know. I want to be a pilot or an astronaut, but I can't decide."

"Either of those would be a good choice. I do believe most astronauts know how to fly."

Henry broke in. "I had to help Lionel with his math once. I don't think he'll make flying school."

"Come on," Tiffany said. "Don't talk to our grandson as if he's already a failure. He's only seven. He has a lot of time to learn math."

Henry ignored her. "Don't fill his mind with dreams, Granny. It's no use planning to fly high if you don't have the intelligence for it. When he's old, he'll understand."

Lionel ran away from the table. Annaliz could see tears in the child's eyes.

There is that word again. Do we ever get away from it? When we're young we're told we're not old enough to do things and, when we get old, we're told we are too old to do them.

As far as I'm concerned, 'old' is like one of those nasty 4-letter words.

Along with them, it should be banned from the dictionary.

She followed the boy into his room, sat on his bed, and put her arm around him. "Don't mind the harsh words," she told him. "There were lots of hard words said to me when I was young, but I didn't let them stop me from doing what I decided was right for me. I made plans. You must do the same."

Lionel smiled through his tears, "You think I should plan on being a pilot?"

"All I know is this. You're only seven. There are many years before you can get a license to fly. Until then, read books and study everything you can find on flying and on being an astronaut. Get ready and the rest will be easy."

He looked up at her. "Did you cry sometimes, Grandma, at the hard words?"

"Oh, yes, my dear. I've cried buckets full."

He laughed aloud and protested, "Nobody can cry a bucket full."

She grinned at him and gave him a hug. "Well, would you believe half a bucket full?"

Back in the family room, in her recliner, she settled down to listen to her relatives discussing their affairs.

She had always liked this comfortable living area. The fireplace filled one wall and bookcases another. The lighting was low and the pictures of farm scenes gave the room a rustic, homey feeling. The far end had a huge farm table, where all the family could gather to have meals. I liked those times the best. When the kids were little it was a joy to see every one around the table at the same time. Is it possible there were really twelve at the table at...? Slowly she sank into sleep.

She was embarrassed when she woke. She had not intended to sleep in her chair. Sleeping like that was for old people, not her. No one was looking at her, at the moment, so she told herself no one had noticed.

Even if they did, it's been a trying week. I'm worn out. Everyone else is too.

In a few days the house grew quiet as visitors left.

Karen cornered Annaliz in the living room with another list of reasons why she should stay in Cameron, instead of going back.

"It's your home here, Mom. You know we'd take good care of you. Why do you want to stay so far away? You need your family. Why just the other day I noticed you were sleeping in your chair in the afternoon. That surely is a sign you should have people around you."

"So they can be sure I haven't died sitting there?"

Morgan, who had come quietly into the room, said sternly, "Aunt Karen, let Grandma live wherever she wants to.

I've been thinking of doing the same thing."

"What? You're moving to Mexico?"

"No, silly. I'm going to go away. I don't know where yet, but I'll figure it out."

"Wait until your mother hears of this," Karen said. "You won't be going anywhere."

"I happen to be 21 and can do what I like."

"Where will you get the money?"

"I saved some for my honeymoon." Her breath caught in her throat. She added. "Also, everyone gave me money for my wedding."

"Well. You can't use it. You didn't get married."

"What difference does it make?" Annaliz broke in.

"They wanted her to have it. It's hers, to do with as she pleases."

Karen spoke sharply. "So she can run away, as you did? Is that what you're telling her?"

Annaliz looked at her in dismay. "You still resent my going to Mexico all those years ago?"

"Of course I resent it. You left when I was about to have Peter."

"Your fifth child."

"Why didn't you stay? A woman needs her mother at such a time. Looking back I believe you were never where I needed you to be. How could you treat me so badly?"

"For one thing I didn't feel you should have a fifth. The overpopulation, even then, was enormous. The cost of a college education was going through the roof. How could the world feed so many people? One day we're going to run out of farmland and then what?"

She took a breath. "Any woman bringing more than two children into this world ought to have her head examined. You already had four. You didn't need another one. Being married at sixteen doesn't give anyone a license to keep on having kids."

Karen said. "You've been pro-choice forever. Well, I believe every child should have a right to live."

"Of course they do, if they're already viable. I'm talking about something else. I'm talking of you getting pregnant on purpose, when you already had more than enough. I didn't like you then."

"So, you think Peter should never have been born?"

"Don't try to lay a guilt trip on me, Karen. Of course I love my grandson and I'm glad he's here. He's a sweet man."

She added, "Why are we talking about the past? It's over and done with. Morgan and I are interested in the present."

Karen said, "I don't understand how you can approve of her running away."

"I don't think she is running away. I think she's running to, and I'm glad." Annaliz threw out her arms in a happy gesture. "I want her to have a little fun while she's young enough to enjoy it."

"And just what is your definition of fun?" Karen had folded her arms across her chest. "You're always using that word. None of the older people in our family say they have fun. Every woman I know, your age, is planning her funeral."

She stomped her foot and rushed on. "It's just plain silly. At your age you should be thinking of more serious things. You keep saying, 'Have fun.' I don't know what you mean."

"Oh, Karen, that's because you've never allowed yourself to have any. Fun is what gets you out of your rut.

Fun is laughter, belly laughter; something to bring tears to your eyes and gaiety to your heart. It's doing something different than you did yesterday, something that turns you on, as the kids would say."

She continued. "It's watching in awe as the sun goes down. It's sharing a moment of laughter with someone you care about. It's smiling at nothing and everything. It's making new friends and yes, it's attempting to absorb new cultures."

She paused for breath. Karen had turned her head away, but Morgan was smiling and wiping tears from her eyes. "I could go on, but you know what I mean. Fun means to be aware, to live each moment as though it may be your last, to appreciate all the wonders waiting for you out there, and there are always new wonders, if you look for them."

Annaliz shook her head. "Fun is to really see your world in a new light every day. Have you ever tried that? Someone said, 'Art is in the details', and I know many people who can't grasp such a concept: people who live in the world without ever noticing it. Well, I'm not one of them and I don't think Morgan is either."

Morgan yelled, "Yeah! Grandma. Let's go get high."

Annaliz laughed until she cried, then said, "If you're living life to the fullest there's no need for another kind of high."

6

Relieved to be back in Mazatlan, Annaliz stopped at the Shrimp Bucket for a quick meal. They made a great Caesar salad, which was her choice for lunch. The restaurant was the favorite of many residents and at one o'clock in the afternoon it was difficult to find a parking space within three or four blocks.

She parked by the bank and sauntered along the sea wall, enjoying the sunshine and the runners. This was a popular place with local runners, because the wall, or malecon, as it was called, ran for over seven miles and they did not have to cross any intersections along the way.

The Shrimp Bucket was in the old La Siesta Hotel, where she had stayed when she first came to Mazatlan. It had expanded and now took up most of the first floor.

Her favorite place to sit was in the patio area, where the band played and the trees and plants gave a garden feeling. She could look up and see the blue sky through the branches of the trees. Now and then she saw a sparrow drift down to the floor to pick up crumbs.

It was always fun to eat at The Bucket, as the locals called it. Annaliz knew if she went further inside she could enjoy the paper flowers and fish on the ceiling and the pictures on the walls of famous fishermen.

Many of her friends also came there for lunch. She looked for someone who could fill her in on all the latest gossip. I must be early, she thought. I don't see the usual crowd. Oh, I know, there's a convention in town and the regulars stay away when so many out-of-towners come.

Weaving her way through the restaurant, stopping here and there to speak to business acquaintances, she finally found a table and was sitting down when she heard her name called. The voice was hesitant, as if unsure. She turned, saw who it was, stood up and held out her arms. "Pancho. How great to see you."

They exchanged hugs, then he said, "My God, Annaliz, you haven't changed a bit."

"You've always been a kidder," she said with a grin. "You haven't changed either. Your smile is just as I remember it. Do you ever stop smiling?"

Pancho said, "I have reason to smile all the time. Remember, thirty years ago, when I left to go to Mexico City, you told me never to marry until I found someone who would be the delight of my life? Well," he turned to the table. "Here she is. My wife, Isabella."

He said. "My love, this is Annaliz."

A beautiful, dark-eyed, smiling woman waved her to a seat. "I've heard so much about you." Isabella said.

Taking a chair, Annaliz pretended to frown. "And what tall tales has he been telling about me?"

Isabella said seriously. "He owes you a great deal."

"For one thing," Pancho said. "I would never have gone to Mexico City. I really was needed there. My family were trying to sell real estate but didn't know the modern ways to go about it. They welcomed me."

He stopped talking for a moment and looked at his wife. "Do you realize I met Isabella the second week I was there? She walked into my office, looking for an apartment. I knew she was the one the minute I saw her. She is so beautiful."

He smiled at his wife and patted her hand. "Do you realize, if I hadn't gone when I did, I wouldn't have been in the office and probably never would have found Isabella. My life would have been ruined."

"Nonsense," Annaliz said. "You would have gone on your own eventually. Since Isabella is your destiny, you would have met somehow, somewhere."

Pancho looked at his wife. "That's what Annaliz believes and she made a believer out of me. She kept telling me I was destined to live in Mexico City. She said my family were there and I should be with them, not in Mazatlan.

He added, "She was right, of course, but I didn't want to believe her. When she kept telling me to go where my heart and mind knew would be the best for me, I thought she had another man and was just trying to get rid of me."

He laughed. "All she was doing was shoving me in the direction I knew I should go."

"I didn't shove." Annaliz said.

"Maybe a gentle push?"

"But it did turn out successfully? You are the big business man now? You are here for the Real Estate convention?"

"Yes. I have two offices in Mexico City and am doing very well indeed. My two sons have taken over much of the work. Isabella and I now have time to take a vacation or come to a convention."

He looked at Annaliz and shook his head. "I worked for so many years without thinking about it. Now I am old, and I understand. If you hadn't given me money and pushed me a little, I never would have accomplished anything."

Ignoring his talk of money, Annaliz said. "You're not old. You're young. You can't be more than 65."

"Hey." He said. "How you do go on. I'm only seven years younger than you. I'm getting up there."

"I've never understood that phrase," she said. "What are you getting up to? Not a lot of mischief, I hope," adding, "if it's to get to some special age,

I'm glad I never got up there. I'm no older now than the day you left."

"I believe you. I know it's the spirit that counts and yours will never be old."

Annaliz grinned at him. "Well, not if I can help it."

She went on. "Maybe I shouldn't have sent you to the City. You missed out on the opportunities here in Mazatlan. About ten years after you left, the tourists came, buying homes and running up the price of real estate."

Laughing, she said. "Because of it, my houses sold for a lot more than I thought they would. I got in on it even if you didn't."

"I got in on it in a way." He said. "My nephew, Carlos, was expert at selling so I helped him open an office in the Golden Zone, and he's done well."

"I can see why. Tourists who come to the Golden Zone spend money as if there's no tomorrow. That's why it's called golden."

She looked at him and asked, with a smile, "So. You gave someone a small push?"

"I learned it from you." Pancho patted her hand. "You told me not to send the money back, but to pass it on, and I did." He looked around. "I help people along now, if I can. In fact I brought two young salesmen with me. They're here somewhere. A convention can teach them things it took me a long time to learn."

He added, "Are you still pushing people into doing something, when they can't decide what they should do or what kind of life they really want?"

"I don't push." She smiled. "I suppose I'm still trying to help people decide what they want out of life. I show them the options. I only want them to live a little, to have fun. I just open the book. It's up to them whether or not they read. Most people's lives are so dull, so flat. What is the harm in trying to do a little something to lift their spirits?"

Pancho said to Isabella, "This woman's spirits are always up. I've never known her to worry about tomorrow. When we were young she swore she would never age and I can see she meant it."

He turned to Annaliz. "Are you still buying old dilapidated houses and fixing them up? I remember that first house." He smiled at the memory. "I was sure you had made a mistake buying it but you showed me how beautiful it could be."

"Well. I'm through remodeling. I did nine of them over the past 30 years. Nine should be enough, don't you think? I also took time out to write a book of poetry and I've been teaching some would-be poets."

Thoughtfully she said, "I seem to be busy every day. I find there are so many interesting things to do and so many plans to make, I don't really have time to work on a house."

"You had a book of poems published? I would like to have a copy."

She grinned at him. "Come on, Pancho. You were never into poetry, as I remember."

"Maybe not," he said laughing, 'but I'd like to show people I know a celebrity."

"I'm no longer a celebrity, if I ever was one. The book was published over ten years ago. I'm not sure if it's still in print."

"I'd like to have a copy if you could find me one."

Isabella leaned towards her. "You must have had an interesting life. What brought you the most joy?"

"Talking and laughing with friends like you and Pancho, I think."

Going home in the afternoon she began thinking of when she had first met Pancho and bought her first run-down house. He tried to persuade me to look at other places but the orange tree in bloom, in what I then called the back yard and is now the patio, was to me a sign of good luck. I wouldn't budge from my decision.

He had been the darling of the real estate office. I remember I watched as every woman who worked there tried to interest him. One woman said he had the most beautiful brown eyes and she wanted them for her children. Another said he was the most compassionate man she had ever known. She didn't care if he had brown or blue eyes, she wanted someone who would be kind to her and she knew Pancho would be.

I don't know if he chose me because I was American and different, or because we laughed together at just about everything. He said he had never met a woman who had such a marvelous laugh. I wonder if I still laugh like that?

He was very helpful when I needed workmen to tile a floor, put in a sink, or repair a fireplace. I needed his aid because he spoke both Spanish and English and the workmen understood him. The work was finished in half the time because of his help.

I knew little Spanish and it was laughable the errors I would have made had it not been for him. I once told a workman I needed a new seat for the toilet and when he returned he had the whole porcelain thing to install.

It took Pancho's help to let him know I had asked for the wrong thing.

When I was young I had difficulty making friends because I was shy. After I was married the only friends I knew were my husband's. Having any of my own was discouraged.

Pancho would have none of this. He taught me most people wanted to be friends with me. He said they were searching for companionship as much as I was. All I had to do was reach out my hand. They were just waiting for me to make the first move.

With him I didn't have to make the first move. He did. He invited me to dinner several times, showed me the city and became my friend. One Sunday he took me to the bullfight. I didn't like it. I thought it too gory.

He said, "Perhaps I shouldn't have taken you, but I think anyone living in Mexico should go at least once. After all, it is part of the local culture."

When I mentioned in the office that I thought the bullfight was too gory, one of the women said, "What do you care if it was gory? You were with Pancho weren't you?" I think they were a bit jealous of me.

I had known him about a year before we made love. That happened in Copala, a little town in the hills, where we had gone for a holiday. It was about 40 miles away on a twisting mountain road. He said he would like to show it to me because, in his mind, the town had the most romantic hotel he knew of, and it was not too far to go on a weekend.

93

Copala was ancient, over 400 years old. It had once been a silver mining town and, evidently, when the price of silver dropped, the town went into decline.

We were told the hotel was over a hundred years old. It really looked it. Vines covered the veranda and had been there for almost as long as the hotel. They had intertwined around the porch supports until I couldn't tell if they or the beams were holding up the roof.

The townspeople had tried to restore the rest of the town so the tourists would come, but they didn't touch the hotel except to add bathrooms. I was glad no one tried to change it. I don't mean I'm into antique hotels, but I like buildings covered with vines. Sometimes I like to try to live in the previous century, just to get a bird's-eye-view of what life could have been like back then. I don't think I would have liked it. It would have been too primitive for me. I do like my creature comforts.

Pancho and I, however, delighted in the little room with a light cord hanging from the ceiling with a 40-watt bulb. We laughed to see that the small closet had been used to make a bathroom. Since there was nowhere to hang clothing we left it in our suitcases.

The balcony gave us a glimpse of the whole town. At night the plaza filled with people, just walking around, drinking coke and beer and talking. Watching, I thought, if there were no cokes or beer bottles available, and the clothing were a little different, this could be a scene from 400 years ago.

Pancho made life fun all the time. He was willing to try anything, but I wasn't so sure about some things. When we went down to dinner he said I should try ceviche. I said I had heard of it and didn't think I would like raw fish.

He said, "It isn't raw. It's cooked in lime juice."

I had never heard of cooking something with juice and was almost afraid to try it. After just one bite I was smitten. It was the best fish cocktail I had ever had. With the fish were chopped tomato, onion, green pepper and a touch of cilantro. One serving didn't seem enough.

Copala is known for having the best banana-cream pie available anywhere in Mexico so the next day we went to a restaurant, high on the hill above the mineshafts, and ate pie. It lived up to its reputation.

Since Pancho was the first man I had even thought of having sex with since my divorce, I wasn't sure exactly how to act the first night but he made loving me seem the natural thing to do.

I had no idea laughter and talk could be a part of having sex. We lay awake for a long time, cuddled in each other's arms, laughing at the silly things happening in our lives and telling each other our innermost thoughts. It was a wonderful night.

I had never been able to laugh or talk, during sex, when I was married. Darrell thought sex was necessary but was meant to be over with as fast as possible, for nothing should interfere with his need for sleep. I realized, after my divorce, that he was already tired from having sex at noon with one of his women.

The first night with Pancho, all the bad sex I'd had in my marriage just disappeared. I found I enjoyed making love. I looked forward to the next time, which I had never done before.

Annaliz smiled, remembering, and thought, Thank you, Pancho, for teaching me sex is not something to be gotten through with quickly, but something to be savored.

Thank you for showing me sex is one way to let someone know they are loved and cared for.

You said, "Sex was invented originally to keep the species growing but whoever designed it knew it was also made to be enjoyed." and I thought, I guess God knew what he was doing.

7

On the way to the public market the next day Annaliz remembered the first time she saw the place. Pancho showed me the city and introduced me to people-watching in the market.

In downtown Mazatlan there were Mexicans of all ages, most of them dressed in bright colors, rushing from one side of the street to the other, calling greetings I couldn't understand.

Even though the language was foreign, I felt I had come home. This was the place I was meant to be. My heart turned over every time I saw the beautiful tiled walls on the sides of the buildings. Arched doorways were everywhere. Had I been a Mexican or a Spaniard in a previous life?

I had no idea if reincarnation happened or not. Now I hope it does. I'd like to think I could be recycled, like a perennial flower, dying in the winter and coming to life again when the sun begins to shine.

At first, I thought no Mexican women used plain colors for all I saw was pattern after pattern. Later I realized the young women loved patterns but older ones dressed quite somberly in plain dark colors. I suppose I should dress as they do but I love color. I wish I could be as flamboyant as Estrella. I just don't have the nerve. I do like green. I wear it anytime I can. Some say it brings out the color of my eyes. I'm vain enough to relish it when someone says I look great in green.

Unable to resist the fabric shop, Annaliz went in and wandered up and down the aisles. There were several pieces she liked. She took her time and finally chose three meters of lime-green linen to have a dress made.

Annaliz giggled as she thought of the astonished look there would be on the dress-maker's face when she walked in. This will be the first time in more than a year, that I've shown up with material for a dress. I'm sure she has given up on me ever being a customer again.

She was crossing the street when, looking up, she saw Estrella coming towards her, her arms full of clothing.

"What in the world are you doing?" she asked.

"Cleaning my closets," Her friend laughed and gave her the usual kiss on the cheek. "I do this once a year. If I haven't worn a piece in the last season I give it away, hoping someone else can get some good out of it."

"What a wonderful idea. I like to see you're recycling things. Where do you take the clothing?"

Thinking of the type of dresses Estrella wore, Annaliz assumed there would be a store specializing in evening clothes.

Estrella said, "There are several charities in Mazatlan happy to have them. I usually go to the Salvation Army. They help families and with my height, it isn't easy to find someone who will fit into these things. I think they can usually find someone who can use them."

"With the number of clothes you have there, it's a wonder you have anything left in your closet."

Estrella said. "Pedro laid down the law. He said if I didn't give him some room in the closet he was leaving me. I really have many more clothes than I need. I should do this every three months instead of once a year."

She put her hand on the clothes. "I am always buying new things; not because I need them but just because I love to shop. You should have something to give. Why don't you clean out your closet?"

Ruefully Annaliz said, "If you noticed what I wore, when we were together, you would know I wear the same thing until it is no good for anything but rags."

"Why in the world don't you buy things? You can certainly afford to, and surely your daughters give you dresses and other clothes for birthdays and Christmas. Didn't Karen give you a gray suit your last birthday?"

"Yeah, she did. Can you imagine me in a gray suit? I buried it as far back in the closet as I could."

Estrella laughed, "I kind of thought you'd hide it. I've never seen you wear a suit. But you astonish me. It's true I never noticed your clothes. Do you mean to say none of your things are new?"

She looked at Annaliz and said, "You've always been clean and neat. I think I would have noticed otherwise, and what you wear seems to fit your personality, so I didn't pay attention. Believe me, from now on I will."

"Sorry I told you," Annaliz said. "Now I'm going to feel as though I'm on parade around you. The truth is, there are certain things I like and don't want to give up."

"Pedro says the same thing. I can't throw out one of his t-shirts. He says it brings him good luck on the golf course."

"I don't know about good luck," Annaliz said, "but I hate to spend money on clothes or other things if what I have is still adequate. I have enough of them to be comfortable and I don't need much. In fact, in the last few years I've begun to buy less and less, feeling I'll probably not wear out what I already have."

She grinned. "I have a plan to rotate things. I don't wear the same thing every day, so I don't get tired of it."

"Oh, for heaven's sake, Annaliz. I can see I will have to take you with me the next time I go shopping. You need some new clothes. You always said you were going to live until you were 120. You'll need many more things. You can't wear the same dress for another 40 years."

They both laughed at these words. Her friend gave her a hug and went on her way.

Annaliz chuckled, thinking of the people at the Salvation Army who would shake out and hang up Estrella's used clothing. Who would buy them? Who would even want them? Who would have courage enough to wear something with sequins or feathers? I suppose they might be purchased for a costume party but I think those fancy clothes will probably be the seven-day-wonder of the Army's shop.

The market was and is my favorite place, she thought, as she looked around. It seems more alive than anywhere else in the world. People are everywhere, buying and selling clothing, leather goods, t-shirts, jewelry and food.

There are shouts from the venders, trying to pull in the customers, and the selling goes on at every booth. It still is as exciting for me today as it was when I first came.

Just like it was years before, bargaining is something the merchants enjoy. They love to haggle with the customer over every little item. Someone might complain 'this particular shirt has a spot on it' and the vender would quickly bring out another and explain, with a smile, how he had been willing to sell the first one cheap because it had a spot.

"But look at this one." He would hold it up. "See, no spots. This one is worth a lot more."

She knew, if you liked to bargain, this was the place to try your skills. I wasn't very good at bargaining in the beginning but now I think I can get my price if I want to bad enough.

In one booth she saw oranges piled so high she couldn't see the top. In another a skinned, boiled, pig's head sat on a counter. The eyes looked out at the people going by. It didn't faze her. She looked right back at it.

One counter sold chickens with the feet still on; some with feathers still on. Annaliz knew if she wanted to make good chicken soup she would include the feet, when she bought her chicken. The feet brought a lot of fat and flavor to her pot.

On a counter in the next aisle she saw shrimp, fresh from the sea and piled high. I'm glad I got here early today. If I'm not here by ten o'clock the fresh shrimp are gone.

Mazatlan is the shrimp capital of the world, and it does send shrimp around the globe, but the local people love it and get first pick when the shrimp boats come in.

Across the street from the market were the flower stands. She always bought flowers when she shopped, even though she grew some herself. The flowers were fresh from the fields and she enjoyed talking to the farmer's wives, who tended the booths.

After years of coming to the same stall, the people knew her and would wave or come give her a hug. She felt at home. Not like the big grocery chains where the turnover in employees was so fast she never knew anyone.

The only reason to ever go to the supermarket, she thought, was to buy canned goods and paper things. Everything else was available fresh from the fields and factories right in the downtown market.

At the farmer's market she could buy vegetables really fresh, instead of at the supermarkets where even celery was so limp she thought it must have been left out in the sun too long.

She thought, I have shopped this same market for over 30 years and know every nook and cranny; where to buy needles and thread; where to pick up a scrap to make a Christmas ornament and where to find a chair to sit when I'm tired. Chairs are in short supply, but one always seems to appear when I stop by.

She remembered the first time she'd walked through the market. The raw meat displayed on tables where people were going by, stirring up dust, made her turn away horrified. The pig's head had left her breathless for a moment. She had smelled the fish counter about 15 feet away and was sure she would never eat fish again.

Years passed. The market was the same but her attitude had changed.

A side of beef was hung three feet behind a counter.

If she wanted to she could have reached across and almost touched it. Then, she would have shuddered at the idea. Now, she said to the butcher, "I'll have that steak," and pointed to within a few inches of it. Neither she, nor the butcher, thought anything of it.

When she first came, years before, the idea of drinking fresh-squeezed orange juice right there in the market, where the floors were dirty and the counters dusty, was a no, no. Now she loved it. Nothing tasted as sweet.

She crossed the busy street once again and went into the shoe store. She didn't really need another pair but she loved shoes. Her closet was full of them, she knew.

I don't spend money on clothes, she thought, but I can't resist a new pair of shoes. She chose a pair of green sandals and asked to have them put in a plastic grocery bag she carried with her.

Aurelia is always chastising me for buying more shoes. She says I have too many now and I don't want to give her another reason to yell at me. If I put them in a grocery bag I can put them away without her seeing them.

She finished her shopping and hopped into a Pulmonia to go home. This cab was like a golf cart, with a bigger motor. No windows, just fresh air. It was called a Pulmonia because, if the weather turned bad, you could catch pneumonia.

The driver carried her grocery bags into the patio and stopped to admire the flowers. The drivers knew she was grateful if they brought in her packages. Since she loved to have her flower-growing abilities praised, she had given each driver a large tip each time they brought her home.

She began taking food from the packages and suddenly, feeling faint, dropped into a chair. Her legs were tingling, as though they weren't getting enough blood and her head felt full, as though she had too much blood there.

Am I having a stroke? Is this how it happens? Damn. I've made other plans. I want to be dancing when it comes.

No. It can't be a stroke. They hit suddenly and hard, without any warning. I remember when Dad had one. He was just sitting talking and the next thing we knew he had collapsed in his chair. We rushed him to the hospital and, although he didn't die from it, he had many months of rehabilitation - in a nursing home, of course.

Dear God. I hope it doesn't happen to me. Dammit. I only spent two hours at the market. Why should I feel so strange? Should I call the doctor?

She sat for more than an hour, wondering why she felt the way she did. She was afraid to get up from the chair, in case she fainted. Gradually her legs became legs again and although her head still felt full, she didn't feel anything fatal was happening. Good, she said to herself. It was nothing.

I won't tell the girls. They would scramble around, getting me ready to go back into a nursing home. No way am I going there. I have other plans.

When I was home for Morgan's wedding, no one, except the bride, remembered it was my birthday. I thought, at the time, they keep telling me I'm too old to stay alone but they pay no attention to each passing year. I guess, if it can't be divided by five it doesn't count. She giggled. If I figured my age their way I'd only be twenty-five or thirty.

Well, she said to herself, if I can laugh at a time like this, things aren't too bad. If I just take it easy next time I go, and try not to do too much, I'll be all right. She did no more and when the maid arrived, Annaliz let her put away her purchases. Aurilia didn't say anything about the shoes. She must have seen I wasn't feeling too well.

When Annaliz went to bed she said aloud, "See. There was nothing wrong. I was just tired."

The episode lingered in her mind for many days. It didn't really slow her down but made her realize there were times when she couldn't do as much as she would like. Just one more reminder of how vulnerable I am, at 78. There is nothing I can do about it but live with it.

Feeling her age, for the first time in a long time, she wanted to cry.

The following day, as she gave herself a good talking to about never giving up, she said aloud, "Yesterday I knew what it felt like to be ancient and I didn't like it. Except for that silly episode, I feel inside as though I'm only 65 but am I kidding myself? Will I drop dead in the market one of these days?"

She thought, well, I'm not going to dwell on it. What will be will be. I'll just enjoy each day as it comes. If I keep a positive attitude, nothing can get me down for long.

A couple of weeks later she had the same feelings. I know how to handle this, she reassured herself, and sat quietly, waiting for it to disappear. When finally, after a little more than hour, it subsided, she muttered, "See. I do know how to take care of it. It's nothing to worry about."

She pretended the thought of having it happen another time wouldn't bother her, but she was hesitant now to try to do too many things in one day. She paced herself so she wouldn't get too tired. She was sure this was what was causing the blood to rush to her head.

I've been lax in taking an aspirin every day. I hate swallowing pills but I must start again. The doctor said I have a healthy heart so it must just be a couple of clogged arteries. Aspirin is supposed to thin the blood so taking the pills will handle the problem.

My body keeps telling me there's nothing to worry about and, after all these years, I trust it to give me a warning if something is really wrong.

Perhaps these are just small strokes. They don't mean anything. They may be telling me to slow down and of course I have slowed down. I know full well I can't do all the things I once did. I would be foolish not to realize it and I may be old but I'm not a fool.

It wasn't hard to take it easy because John was gone much of the time.

When he was home they seldom had times for dances. She didn't tell him of her strange feelings. She didn't want to worry him with something she could handle by herself and the thought of letting her daughters know about these episodes never entered her mind.

8

John was in town the next day and she woke up feeling as though she could fight the world. I have to do something to make this day worthwhile, she thought. I know. I'll make some ceviche for our dinner. She put on an apron and was in her sunny kitchen chopping onions, tomatoes and green peppers to make salsa, when Karen called.

Without even saying hello, she asked belligerently, "What have you done to Tiffany?"

"Tiffany?" What was Karen talking about?

"I haven't done anything," Annaliz said, "What's wrong? Is she ill?"

"She's going back to school."

"For heaven's sake why do you sound mad? I'm glad to hear it. It will

117

be good for her. It's time she branched out a bit."

"Henry called me. He doesn't think it's a good idea. He's ready to have a fit. He thinks it's silly to go to school when you're almost 50 years old, and he doesn't like the thought of her being gone in the evenings."

"He should go back to school. He needs to grow a little. People of all ages are in school these days and I'm glad to see it. One can never have enough education."

"He's mad because Tiffany told him you put her up to it. How could you do it without consulting Henry?"

"For Pete's sake, why should I ask him? He's not the one who asked me what she should do. You mean Tiffany has to ask his permission before she can do anything? How silly. She's old enough to make up her own mind. Why in the world should he care how she spends her evenings? He's out bowling a lot from what she says."

Karen said, "I think husbands should be in on the decision. After all, it takes time away from her time with him. What did you tell her anyway?"

"I told her if she wanted to write something, she should get a teacher. Anytime we try something new we need help. It's the smart thing for her to do."

"She's trying to write poetry." Her mother could hear the scorn in Karen's voice.

Annaliz wondered, why is it she can't be happy for someone else who is trying to grow a little? She seems to feel each of us should stay in our little rut and never venture beyond it. It would be nice if, for once, she could be helpful instead of sounding jealous.

Did she feel the same when my book of poetry came out? Was she envious of me? Has she disliked me ever since? Can that be the reason she is forever trying to make me do something I don't want to do?

119

How could I have two girls, raised in the same environment, so totally different? Tiffany seems delighted whenever something good is happening to someone else.

Was there something I did to create this difference in my daughters? Did I show favoritism to Tiffany because she was the baby? I remember I tried not to, but she was a much happier child than Karen, who always had a chip on her shoulder.

"I'm glad Tiffany's going to school. I think it's wonderful." Annaliz said. "I'm sure she'll be good at poetry. Don't you remember? English was her favorite class in high school."

Karen heard her mother's voice rise in what she called her 'getting ready to pounce' mode, as Annaliz added, "and what are you doing to improve yourself?"

There was a long pause. "If you must know, I'm painting again."

"Wonderful. I remember you were very good at it in college. I wondered why you didn't keep it up."

"Edgar didn't want me to. He said he needed me in the business. He said art didn't pay."

Annaliz thought, I don't think he cared whether it paid or not. He just wanted to control what Karen was doing. She could never really be the boss when he was around.

Why is it husbands think they should have a say when their wives want to do something they can't do? Why is being the boss so important to them? Someone made a serious mistake when they decided one gender should be in charge.

Answering the question she thought Karen was trying to ask, Annaliz said, "Sometimes art pays and sometimes it doesn't. What's important is, when you're doing something you love, you get a satisfied feeling. You can't put a price on that."

"Then you think I should keep on with it?"

"Of course, my dear. If you enjoy it you must keep on. Tell Edgar it's just a hobby. Lord knows he doesn't need you in the business anymore. Tell him all his friend's wives have a hobby; you're just following the local trend. He'll leave you alone then."

Karen laughed, the first time her mother had heard her laugh in a long time. "You certainly have Edgar down pat. How come you can read people so well?"

"Hang on a second, dear. I'm slicing tomatoes and the juice is running all over."

She took a few minutes to put the tomatoes in a bowl and wipe up the mess, then said, "To answer your question: I have a few more years than you and one does learn some things with age. I've known him almost as long as you have."

She added, "What are you painting? You used to do beautiful landscapes. Remember the one you gave me on my 60th birthday? I've always treasured it. It gives me a feeling of home to see the birch trees."

"That old thing?" Karen said. "You still have that?"

"Of course, I love it, but I'd like to see some of your new work. I'm sure it will be beautiful. Let me know when you have your first gallery showing. I'll be there."

Karen giggled. "Oh, Mom, it will never happen."

"But it might."

What a nice giggle, Annaliz thought. It sounds like the young Karen I remember. Painting must be therapy for her. It must be making her happy and I know she hasn't felt happy for a long time. I do hope she keeps on with it.

"You'll be the first to know if I'm ever invited to show in a gallery," Karen said, "but I'm not into landscapes right now. I'm trying my hand at something entirely new. Since I don't know myself how it will turn out, I can't tell you much about it."

She laughed. "It's become an obsession with me, though, to really work at it. I know I'm neglecting Edgar. I have a studio downtown and work there every day. I'm excited about this painting. It's going to be totally different from my other work."

"I can't wait to see it."

When Karen hung up Annaliz thought, I could draw a little when I was young. I drew pictures of everyone I could get to sit still. Portraits came easy to me. I liked doing it. One teacher even said I had possibilities.

She sighed. I did keep at it until I married. Somehow, there was never enough time after the wedding, and if I did try to paint someone I was laughed at and asked if I thought I was an artist.

I don't know why I ended up being a poet in Mazatlan, instead of an artist.

Perhaps, when I got here, I saw so much beauty, I felt I had to express how I felt about it and couldn't do it well enough with a paintbrush.

Maybe my love of words inspired me. The teacher who taught me English in the sixth grade helped me realize how important words were in our lives. She told us, "The right words help you make friends. The correct use of words can make your descriptions come alive for others. If you want to be an author, you will learn each word is important, no matter how simple your sentence may seem."

She then looked at us with a smile and said, "And if you want to write poetry, each word must come from the heart."

When I was living with Jorge, I realized he used the right words when talking to me. I knew he spoke from the heart. He had an easy way of expressing exactly how he felt and he told me I should write. He said I'd be good at it.

He was my biggest fan. It was easy to write from the heart when he was around.

I love the way words fit the occasion. Just say the word, 'bang' and I hear a sharp explosion. Someone says, 'storm' and in my mind I can see it raging. When I think of 'snow', quiet descends upon me as it used to, when I lived in the north in the winter, and just to hear the word 'joy' fills my soul. I guess I was meant to be a poet.

I should make plans to start writing again but it is so easy to let the days go by and not worry about doing anything constructive.

I was quite active when I first came to Mexico.

I really worked hard for many years at the remodeling jobs. It was creative as well as fun to do. It was like being an artist. I really don't want to do another remodel. Okay, I realize part of the reason may be years have gone by and I don't have the energy I had once. I suppose I could do it if I had to, but just sitting in the sun is making me happy now.

When I fell in love with Jorge, I still kept on with the remodeling but I also wrote the book of poetry. What a labor of love. I'm glad I finished it before he died. I don't think it would ever have gotten done if he hadn't been there to egg me on.

I'm getting lazier as time goes by. No. I will not say it. It is not because I am old. I have always had a tendency toward laziness. I am now taking advantage of being comfortable enough financially to not do anything I don't want to do.

She thought of what she had told Karen; "Contentment is for cows." and had to laugh, to think she might now be a cow in her own pasture, content in her own kitchen. I'll never tell her I'm thinking her way. She would really rub it in and say she was right and I was wrong.

Thinking about it, she knew it wasn't only contentment she felt. It was the excitement of each new day, which Karen did not seem to feel. I still have an enthusiasm for almost every happening in my life. She giggled. And if nothing is happening around me, I go out and look until I find something. I may be growing old but I guess I'll never grow up.

Adding one chopped green chili to the salsa, she placed the bowl in the refrigerator. All I have to do now is stop at the market and pick up some fresh fish and limes and I can make John and me a wonderful bowl of ceviche for dinner.

It's one of our favorite meals: raw fish, marinated in lime juice for four hours, with salsa added at the last hour.

When the family comes I don't offer them this dish. They think raw fish is poison. They do love their tacos, though, so I guess they like some Mexican dishes.

John really likes the local food. He likes it very hot. I have to ask the cook in a restaurant not to put too many chilies in my food because, if I get too much, I start to cough. John wants them loaded onto his plate.

I prefer rice and chicken, because it usually doesn't have a lot of chili in it, and I really like the way they make pasta in one restaurant here. I've never been able to figure out their recipe for Alfredo sauce. The waiters laugh when I ask for it, but it is creamy and full of cheese and some day they will tell me, I'm sure.

John teases me when I ask. He says, "Why learn to make it at home, when your favorite restaurant, that makes it so well, is just down the street?"

He can't understand why I don't especially care for burritos. "What are you doing in Mexico if you don't like the food?" he asked.

"I like some of it," I said. "I like tacos and ceviche, but even at home I had some likes and dislikes. I hate

129

rutabagas, for one thing. Surely I can dislike one thing here."

John laughs with me, not at me, and I enjoy sparring with him.

Out in the back yard, picking flowers for the house, she heard the next-door neighbor watering his lawn. She called across the wall, "Miguel, would you like some flowers? My zinnias are taking over the garden."

"Angelica would love them," he said. "She's at the market right now but when she comes home I'll have her come over. She says you have the most beautiful flowers in the whole town. She wants me to have a garden like yours, but I haven't the slightest idea how to grow flowers."

"It's easy. I'll give you some seeds and some small plants to get started."

"Hey." He laughed. "I didn't say I wanted to have a garden. You have to weed and water. I know how much work it is. My wife doesn't understand. She thinks they just come up on their own.

Don't tell her otherwise or I might have to grow some."

"You're just plain lazy," she said laughing.

"I know, but don't tell her. She thinks I'm wonderful."

As Annaliz went back into the house to arrange the flowers, she thought, Miguel and Angelica are such good neighbors. I know if I needed anything I would only have to ask and they would come help me.

Back home, when I lived in an apartment, after Tiffany and Henry moved into my house, I didn't know my neighbors. The people in the other apartments might nod to me on the stairs, but to actually get to know them meant time had to be taken out of each of our busy schedules, and no one wanted to do it.

Unlike Mexico, people in the States are hesitant to aid others in distress. If something goes wrong they sue each other for any little problem. In Mazatlan, suits of this kind are almost unknown. If bad things happen unintentionally, the locals just pass it off as an accident, an act of God. Suing each other never enters their mind.

Life is much simpler here. Each person seems willing to help another and, when they meet, it's expected a kiss and hug will be given. It means so much more to me than a handshake.

I don't think I knew, before I came down, how much mere acquaintances could add to one's life. I had thought someone had to be a bosom buddy, or the person couldn't really be important to me.

In Mazatlan, strangers on the street smile and nod, the bus and taxi drivers ask your name so they know you next time. I like this casual, friendly way of living.

In some ways, Mexico is living in an era fifty years behind the United States. Then, at home, there was similar compassion among people of all classes.

We took care of each other. When something went wrong, there was usually a neighbor who came to the rescue. If not him, then the church would collect funds or food and clothing to help out. Now, we seem to have lost a sensitivity to another's need.

Mexico is up to date in a great many ways but, thank goodness, they haven't yet become indifferent to their fellow man.

As I thought years ago, I still feel as though I must have been a Mexican or a Spaniard in a previous life, or perhaps I can trace my ancestry all the way back to the local Indians. Maybe I should learn how to do genealogy and see what I can find.

9

Annaliz was leaning against the next-to-last step on a tall stepladder when a loud voice exclaimed, "What the hell are you doing up there?"

Startled enough to almost fall from her perch, she looked around and said, "What's it look like I'm doing, dancing the tango? And what are you doing here? You're not due until tomorrow."

Henry and Edgar stood in the living room doorway, suitcases in hand. Dressed in their 3-piece suits, they looked like the businessmen they were, instead of men on a vacation.

She knew they would never give in to the local custom of wearing shorts and a t-shirt. It was hot out today but she was sure they wouldn't change their attire except to put on golfing togs.

Edgar said, "I heard of a golf tournament I wanted to enter. I thought it started on Saturday but it starts tomorrow instead, so we had to come a day early."

She said, "You might have let me know. I had other plans. I do have a telephone, you know."

Henry said, "I suppose if we'd called, you wouldn't be up there on a twelve foot stepladder painting the living room. You didn't want us to know you would do such a thing."

He took a breath and exhaled noisily. "You're a crazy old woman. I wonder how in hell you've lived as long as you have when you do such stupid things."

She retorted. "I sometimes think it's because I do stupid things, as you call them, that I've been allowed to live this long. I'm having a good time." She glared down at him. "Anyway, I'm not painting the whole room. I'm only painting one wall, and if I want to kill myself I can do so. You ought to try taking a few risks, Henry. Your life is pretty dull, it seems to me."

"It may be dull but it's a lot safer than yours. Get down from there right now."

Annaliz looked down at him. "And if I get down, are you going to finish painting the wall for me?"

"Of course not. I don't do menial work and you shouldn't either. You can afford to hire someone to paint for you."

"I like doing things my way. I want this wall to be a pale green so it will filter the sunlight and make it seem cooler in here."

She added, "Besides, it's more fun if I do it myself."

"There you go again with the word 'fun'. I have talked with Karen about your silly ideas. What you consider fun, we think is stupid. You take risks no one your age should take. You act like a kid sometimes. At 78, I shouldn't have to tell you. You should know better. Having fun is for teenagers."

Annaliz turned back, picked up the paint roller and came down a step. "Go put your stuff away." She said. "You know where your bedroom is. This teenager wants to finish this before the top dries."

Henry, not willing to go until he'd had the last word said, "I know you've been independent all your life. It was what ruined your marriage, but it seems at 78, you should be willing to accept some advice."

"Oh, and what advice is that?"

"Let other people take care of you. You're too old to make decisions for yourself. Being in your second childhood doesn't mean you can act like a child."

Annaliz laughed. "When I was a child I was not allowed to act like one, so I'm making up for it now. I love being in my second childhood. Go away, Henry, and let me have my fun."

Strange, she thought. I haven't thought of my childhood for a long time. My parents died when I was two and life with a grandmother, who didn't approve of a single thing I did, made me rebel against anyone who wanted to give me orders.

Shaking her head, she turned back to the wall. Henry loves to rile me, she thought. I shouldn't let it happen but I can't resist fighting back.

She finished painting, put the ladder away and went to change into clean clothes. She put on a white shirt, some brown short shorts and got out her thongs. If Henry thinks I'm a child I'll show him I can dress like one.

I'm being obnoxious, I know. It's just, I hate it when someone tries to tell me what to do. I know I probably shouldn't feel fussed but Henry always seems to get my back up.

"Don't make lunch for us," Edgar said, as he came into the room, dressed for golf. "We'll eat at the club."

"Good. I didn't have anything planned. I didn't expect you until tomorrow."

"I know." he said. "Sorry. Henry said you were family so we didn't need to call."

Annaliz frowned. "Family or not, a little common courtesy would be welcome."

Edgar said, "Why do you fight with him? I know it's necessary for you to be independent if you're going to live alone. I think it's okay but Henry resents it. He wants everyone to do just what he wants when he wants it. Wouldn't it be easier to just go along, as I do?"

She looked at him, shook her head, and said, "This is one woman who doesn't believe in just going along. I'm going to do what I want and he can just lump it. I am independent. If I wasn't I wouldn't be here in the place I love most in the world. No idiot like Henry is going to drive me away."

She wondered how they thought she'd survived all these years if she couldn't take care of herself. They call it being independent. I call it using common sense. It's true, since my divorce, I have asked for help from no one and I plan to continue to do the same. As far as I'm concerned, if I ever have to give up doing what I want, instead of what someone else wants, I might as well be dead.

Henry came out, stopped in front of the hall mirror to comb his hair, saw Annaliz standing there in her short shorts, and sniffed the air as if he smelled something he didn't like.

He hesitated and then, as if he couldn't help himself said, "My God. Do you know how you look in those things?"

Annaliz, smiling inside, turned toward him and with an innocent look on her face, said, "What things?"

He snarled. "No woman should be seen in shorts that short, much less an old lady like you."

She laughed with glee and said, "These? You should see the really short ones I usually wear."

Edgar, giving both of them a dirty look, pushed Henry out the door.

When the men had gone she shoved the chest she had moved, in order to paint, back against the wall and arranged a bowl of flowers on top of the low bookcase.

Standing back, she admired her handiwork. Looks good. One wall in leaf green sets off the yellow in the room. I like it and it brings the color of the greenery from outside into the house.

She called Ramona to see if their luncheon date was still on. Deciding to change her clothes to something a little more appropriate, she put on the new green dress she'd had made and drove to the Golden Zone.

Ramona had chosen the beach restaurant called La Fiesta to have lunch. Their table was situated on the sand, its legs dug in so it wouldn't tip. The top was pale blue tile and the waiters had tied purple napkins into flower shapes.

Deep blue waves, washing up on the shore within 15 feet of their table, seemed to blend with the décor.

Annaliz said, laughing, "You should have seen me this morning, Ramona. I don't think I was at my best," and she told her of the men coming at the wrong time and catching her on the ladder.

"You should have heard Henry yell. I almost fell off I was so startled. He was his usual obnoxious self and you know he always rubs me the wrong way."

She laughed. "He was right, of course. I did plan to do it when none of the family was here. They weren't supposed to come today. I don't like to have them around when I want to do something I know is risky. They're always so bossy. Every one of them is sure, if I'm left alone, I'm going to do something outrageous. Henry is the worst of all."

Ramona said, "Come on, Annaliz, you know it's really not a good idea to climb a ladder. I haven't climbed one in years. It's dangerous. You should have had a man do it. We women weren't made to climb."

"You mean because of our age?"

"Partly, and the fact your ceilings are fifteen feet high. Too high for someone any age to be in the air, and you know it. Just the slightest misstep and there would be a catastrophe. I know you like to take risks, but ladders should be avoided even by risk takers like you."

"I wasn't that high, silly. I was only up about ten feet."

"Have you thought what a fall from ten feet would do to your body?"

"Of course I know," Annaliz said, "but when I really want something done and no one is around to do it right away I don't think of the consequences. I just go ahead, make plans, and do it. I've found it's the only way. Otherwise I could sit for days waiting for help."

She grinned at Ramona. "And anyway, it's more fun if I do it myself."

Her friend laughed. "And having fun has gotten you into trouble many times, if I remember your stories. Sorry to say this, but Henry is right. You shouldn't do it again."

"Hey," Annaliz objected. "Whose side are you on, anyway? You're just as independent as I am and you take just as many risks. Don't you remember telling me about that weekend you were in San Miguel? Boy! I've heard you tell of worse things than just climbing a stepladder, like I did."

"Yeah." Ramona grinned at the memory. "They were risky, of course, but the things I did then were not done on top of a twelve-foot stepladder."

Laughing together, they spent the afternoon trying to outdo each other telling outrageous things they had done in earlier years.

They finally realized it was almost four o'clock; the waiters were waiting for them to go so they could set up tables for dinner.

Going home after the luncheon, Annaliz thought, what would I do without good women friends like Ramona? We can really let our hair down with each other. Our secrets, the ones we would never tell to a man, are open to other women.

I suppose it's because when we're with a man our mind is asking, 'Do I dare tell him this? Will he like me less if I do? Will he take advantage of me because of it?'

Somehow the sex in the background keeps us from being as honest with a man as we are with our women friends. I don't mean we tell lies - just lies of omission.

We, at least I, can't be as open as I would like with them. It's my independence thing again. I'm afraid if I let men too far into my psyche I'll no longer be me - and being me has been the most important thing in my life since I came to Mazatlan.

For years I lived with no thought of myself, only my husband and children. Funny. I thought, as time went by, they might appreciate it but no one ever did. Instead I was yelled at and beat down until I had no soul of my own, only the 'family'.

I might as well have been a robot for all the notice I was given. I was just supposed to be there, doing my thing, for the rest of my life. Thank God I came to my senses and got out of there.

Moving far away from everyone I had ever known meant I could start being the kind of person I always wanted to be. There was no one to look with scorn if I wanted to write poetry. When I worked, the money was mine, to do with as I wished. When I wanted to buy a piece of run-down property and fix it up, there was no one to say it was a bad idea.

When I was with the family and wanted to spend money buying a bouquet of flowers, to make my surroundings look better, I was told I could not do it. They said the money should be used to buy something useful. I tried to explain I needed a bit of beauty in my life and got laughed at. "For heaven's sake," I was told, "We don't need flowers in the house. If you want beauty, go to church and look at the altar. It has flowers."

Now I can buy all the flowers I want, even grow my own, and no one can tell me no. I can even buy an old run-down chair, like the one I'm sitting in. She had to grin. I can just imagine what I would have been told if I'd tried to do it back then.

Laughing out loud, she thought, now if I don't want to entertain the boss I don't have to. If I decide this year I'm going to eat Thanksgiving dinner at a restaurant I can do that. I believe every year I was married I cooked holiday meals for his family.

They all loved camping and I hated it. I couldn't understand how cooking over an open fire made anything taste better. I would much rather have cooked the meal at home on an electric range. I was terrible at cooking out in the open anyway, and most of the time I ended up with burns on my arms and ashes in my hair.

I guess I've always hated to conform. I wanted to be a free spirit and, once I left Grandma's house, I was one. Living in an apartment alone was Heaven to me. I was never lonely. I was happy until I got married. I didn't realize marriage meant someone would have the right to dictate my every move.

I did what was required. I had two kids. I was a wife. I cooked, cleaned, washed and took the kids to all the extra-curricular activities mothers have to be available to do. I had no time of my own.

I do believe I was constipated until my kids were twelve or so. Every time I wanted to go to the bathroom someone would be at the door yelling they needed me. I never had ten minutes to myself.

I don't dislike my kids for demanding service. I knew, when I decided to get pregnant, I would have to take care of them. I loved them from the beginning but I think I loved them most when they got married. It gave me the freedom I needed to start over.

It took many months of living in Mazatlan to realize I no longer had the responsibilities that had been my life for twenty-two years.

I relaxed. I began to venture out, to make new friends. I bought bright clothing. For once in my life I could wear green without being told it was too much color for a married woman like me.

Laughing at the thought, she said to herself, and I bought a dozen pairs of shoes in one month.

It took me about three months before I began to revel in the knowledge that the only person I was responsible for was me. I felt like a little kid, riding his first bike, who yells, "Hey, Ma. Looka-me. No hands."

She sighed. Dear God, what a relief it was to know I could just be me.

10

The call from Tiffany came at five in the morning. Edgar had died in the night. "Mom, Karen is out of it. I hope you can come. I've never known her to act like this. She's always been the one in charge and now she's wailing like a banshee. I can't stand it." Tiffany began sobbing.

"Ask the doctor to give her a sedative for now, Tiffany. I'll catch the next plane and should be there sometime tonight. Try to get her kids to come home and rally round. It's time they learned to cope in a crisis."

On the plane she remembered, with a smile, Karen at the age of three; bossy and determined to have her way, even then. I should probably have tried to keep her from ordering everyone around, but she was so cute it was hard to slow her down. Over the years, she has become a real martinet. She demands to be the leader so I can see why Tiffany was overwhelmed at her falling apart.

It must have been something more than just Edgar's death causing it. Karen has never been the type to break down in front of other people. Appearances mean everything to her.

Peter picked Annaliz up at the airport. "Mom's still sleeping," he said. "The doc really knocked her out. I haven't been able to talk to her yet."

"Was your dad sick before the heart attack?" she asked. "No one said anything to me."

"He knew he had a bad heart. Mom tried to get him to diet but he wouldn't do it. He was warned if he gained any more weight it might happen."

At the funeral home the night before the memorial, Annaliz looked at the open coffin and thought, I sure hope they don't have mine open when I die. They've prettied Edgar up so he doesn't look like himself.

If they did me in the same way, I think I'd rise right up and scream. I want to be cremated but I guess, even then, there can be a viewing. What an awful word for coming to see someone in his coffin. I don't want anyone to see me after I'm dead.

The next day, looking around at the mourners in the funeral home, where there were more flowers than people, Annaliz realized Edgar was not a popular man.

The family was there, of course. It was expected of them but few business associates filled the other seats.

I don't want to speak ill of the dead but he was a difficult man to know. He was close-mouthed about his business; never went out of his way to make friends, and seemed to shun people who didn't think or act as he did.

Karen was different. She wanted to be the boss but she had many friends who loved her anyway. She changed after they married. They were a strange couple.

It wasn't until after the funeral and the rest of the family had gone home, Annaliz had an opportunity to talk to her daughter alone.

"I killed him," Karen said, her eyes swollen from weeping. "When I was home I watched what he ate. I saw he took his pills, but I've been gone a lot. " She began crying again.

Annaliz tried to put her arms around her daughter but was repulsed.

"No," Karen said, "I don't deserve sympathy. These last few months I've been downtown painting. I've been so engrossed in my art I haven't had time for my husband. I killed him."

She cried. "Even the neighbors think so."

Annaliz said, in as sharp a voice as she could muster. "You did not kill him.

Quit saying such a thing. He was a grown man. He should have taken care of himself. What you did or didn't do for him had nothing to do with it."

Karen wailed, "Then why did he have to die just as I was becoming successful? My painting is to be shown at Laguna next week. Did he die now just to show me I couldn't succeed at anything?"

She screamed, "How can I go to Laguna when my husband has just died? It's not fair."

Oh, dear. Her hysterics were only partly for Edgar's dying. He hadn't wanted her to paint. During their marriage she had pretended to be the boss but her husband really called the shots.

She was finally going to prove to him she could achieve something on her own and now she can't do it. She thinks he has again come out the winner in her continual battle to be the one in charge.

To Karen she said, "You will go to Laguna next week, of course. I will go with you."

She tried to get a smile from her daughter. "Do you remember when you started painting again a few months ago? I told you I would be at your first gallery showing? Well, I'm certainly going to be there."

When Karen didn't smile, she added, "Why didn't you let me know one of your paintings had been accepted?"

"It's not a big gallery and," Karen sobbed, "next week is only for beginners. I didn't think you'd want to come."

She got out a Kleenex and blew her nose, then turned to Annaliz. "It's a juried show, however, so it does have a bit of prestige."

Tears came to her eyes. "I did want Edgar to be there." This time she allowed her mother to give her a hug.

"Of course. Of course. I understand." I understand more than you know, Annaliz mentally told Karen.

Why is it, when someone dies, we all have guilty feelings? It's as though we had somehow let them down, didn't give them enough attention, should have loved them more or, as in this case, needed to vindicate ourselves in their eyes and they deprived us of the opportunity by dying. It happens to all of us.

We don't know whether to cry because they are gone or hate the person for dying and leaving us without warning.

I remember when Jorge died so suddenly. I wept, not for him but for me. I had lied to him about my age. I was really 70 when I told him I was his age of 63.

At his funeral I raged because I didn't have a chance to tell him the truth. There were so many other things I had meant to tell him that morning; the rose bush is in bud, we need to take the cat to the vet; bring milk when you come tonight.

I remember screaming silently at his funeral, "Come back, I need to tell you I love you one more time."

I really loved Jorge. I've often wondered if Karen loved Edgar or only stayed with him because she was competitive and wouldn't leave until she could get the best of him.

What will she do now? Will she be bossier than ever with the rest of us? Death leaves so many unanswered questions.

When I die, I hope I can somehow leave a message saying, "Have no guilt feelings. My love will always be with you. I lived my life as I wanted to. You gave me everything you had to give while I was here. Let me go with loving thoughts."

She got ready to go to the art show. It was more work than she wanted to do and she woke up tired. They each had to have a new dress, and have their hair and nails done.

Annaliz didn't think all this necessary just to go look at some paintings, but Karen kept saying she had to look the part of a successful artist. She said it was expected in California.

Damn. Annaliz knew she should never have agreed to go. She should have made other plans, but she wasn't going to let Karen know anything bothered her. I can't let being tired keep her from this opportunity.

I do hope her painting is a success. She's worried it might not be good enough; it might not show up well with other's work. I have to be with her to help her cope.

How many times over the years have I pretended to feel great and said I was fine, when I wasn't, just because some event was happening the family felt I shouldn't miss?

If I even suggested I might be too tired I was told, "Oh, Grandma. Come on. You can do anything when you really want to. I know you. You can't be too tired to be at my champion ball game."

I would go, of course. I was raised in a family where giving up yourself for others was the right thing to do. Annaliz thought, I was told no matter how you felt, if someone needed you, you must go.

It seems now, pretending has become my way of life. Even when I'm aching in every bone, I try to keep a smile on my face for everyone I meet. I try to never let down my guard. No matter how I feel, I grit my teeth and go on, although I may really be hurting. For some reason I don't want to admit to anyone in the family I could be less than the perfect grandmother.

I know we all put on a different mask with each person we talk to. I try not to do it too much but I do pretend when it comes to my health. I hate to have people hovering around me.

Thank God we flew to California. I don't think I could have stood two or three days driving in the car with Karen, worrying about something at every mile.

"What will I do if no one likes my work?" she asked over and over.

Annaliz laughed. "Just pretend you're painting doesn't belong to you but to some other artist."

Karen was horrified. "Mom, don't laugh. I'm having nightmares."

The gallery, a small one, seemed lost among so many.

The floor was carpeted. A lamp over each painting was the only lighting, giving a soft, inviting glow to the room.

There were only a few people walking through, carrying glasses of champagne, discussing the paintings, as they sauntered by the walls filled with beginner's work.

Karen had gone to talk to the owner of the gallery and left her mother to find her way alone. Some of this is pretty primitive, Annaliz decided. Her picture will surely be better than most of these.

161

Moving along, she at last found her daughter's painting.

It was unlike anything she could have imagined.

Slashes of color filled an otherwise blank canvas. There seemed no reason for some one to paint something like this unless they were in a rage.

And rage it was. Red, orange and a vicious pink vied for attention with dashes of a bilious green.

She had known Karen was an angry woman but, as she stood there, actually feeling it; realizing for the first time how deep it must be, she heard a man on her left say, "Ah. Now here we have something."

He stepped in front of Annaliz to get a better look. Turning to the woman with him, he said, "It has been said, art is in the eye of the beholder, but I believe it's in the heart and soul of the painter. He cannot tell us how he feels and no words are needed. Look at this one. The work says it all."

The woman said. "But, darling, it's such a cruel painting. I wouldn't want to own it. I can't even look at it twice."

"Exactly," the man replied. "This was not done so it could hang on someone's wall to be admired. We usually do not put our souls on display like this. I must have it. There are times when I need to look on another's agony to make me realize I am not alone in this horrible world."

They moved on and left Annaliz staring at the painting. What could have possessed Karen to paint something like this? Why would a gallery owner want to hang it?

Believing it should not be on display, she hurried to the manager of the gallery and said she would like to buy the painting by Karen Simpson.

"I am sorry," he said. "I have two people who already have asked to buy it. The painter does not wish to sell."

"But why not?" she asked. "Isn't it why these beginners show their work? Don't they want to be commercial?"

"Yes, most of them, but some paint for satisfaction alone, and I feel this is one of them."

Annaliz turned away. Karen will want to know what I think of her painting. What am I to say? You should burn it? She didn't think the idea would go over well and yet it was what she felt.

How could her daughter have painted such an obscenity? Was this really what Karen had wanted to show Edgar? Would he have known what it meant?

Do we ever know our own children? Why haven't I been able to see what a very angry woman she is? She has turned me off so many times, by insisting I do what she wants that I've failed to search for her reasons.

Her marriage must have been hell if she had to bring out the truth of it in this way. Have I been neglectful in not digging into her life a little deeper?

And what about Tiffany? Is her need for writing poetry a call for help? Am I a bad mother for not realizing my children's needs?

Stop it! You don't believe in guilt. You've said so often enough. They are grown women. If they wanted help they could have asked for it.

No mother is guilty of neglect after her kids get to the age of eighteen. If she hasn't taught them to think for themselves and fend for themselves by then, she should feel guilty, but not otherwise. I know I taught my girls to be self-sufficient.

Back in the hotel room, Karen was radiant with success. She didn't ask for her mother's opinion. She exclaimed, "There were three people who wanted to buy my painting, Mom. I was afraid it would not do that well."

"Wonderful, dear. What are you asking for it?"

"Oh, I don't intend to sell it."

"For heaven's sake, why not? Don't artists paint so they can sell things?"

"Most of the time yes, but this time I only wanted to see if I could do it. And I did."

In bed, at the hotel in Laguna, waiting for sleep, Annaliz had a horrible thought. What if rage was the only thing Karen had as an artist? Would the next painting be a disaster?

11

Annaliz had been back in Mazatlan about a month when Ramona called. "Are you interested in doing another remodeling?"

"Not really," Annaliz said. "I'm happy in this house. I don't think I'll ever do another. At the moment I don't have any other plans."

"Ha. You're just old and tired and won't admit it."

"Look who's talking, old friend. I haven't noticed you kicking up your heels lately. I'm merely enjoying myself by doing absolutely nothing. I highly recommend it to everyone. I pay no attention to my age. It's only a bunch of meaningless numbers strung together. They don't mean a thing if you don't let them."

Ramona said, "I knew you'd say that, but I've had to let those numbers mean something in the last couple of weeks. I've been feeling terrible."

"I didn't know you were ill, dear. Why didn't you call me? I might have been able to help."

"I suppose I would have, if I'd known what the problem was, but the doctor doesn't know what's wrong and he keeps giving me these pills, a different one each time I go, and they don't do me any good."

Ramona was furious. "Annaliz, do you know what he said last time I was in? He said it was all in my head. I was so mad when I left his office. He had told me not to drink liquor so I went right out and had a Tequila Sunrise."

"Hey!" Annaliz laughed out loud. "What a way to go. Did it help?"

Ramona said dryly, "Well, not really. I knew it wouldn't, at the time, but felt I had to do something. This doctor won't listen to what I say."

"You say 'this doctor'. Do you mean he's a new one?"

"You wouldn't believe how many doctors I've seen in the last few months," she said. "I can't seem to get any satisfaction out of any of them."

She continued, "This one is only saying things about my head because he doesn't want to deal with me any longer. I'm old and have more things wrong with me than young people do. He won't take time to listen to my problems. I think he'd prefer a younger person so he could hand them a pill and they would go away quickly. I always seem to have one more question he doesn't want to answer."

"He is probably right about it being in your head, but not in the way he thinks. It is in your head, but not in your head alone. It's in your whole body. You need to listen to it. Your body can tell you what is wrong but neither you, nor your doctor, are interested in hearing what it's saying. Instead, you accept a new pill, like the young adults do, not even asking what it is supposed to do for you, and you come home and within a few hours feel worse than when you went in. Take a moment and let your body tell you where you hurt."

"Do you mean you listen to your body?" Ramona asked. "It sounds kind of silly but I know you are never ill for long. Is that your secret?"

"Yes, but it's no secret. I've been trying to get people our age to do this for years."

"How do you go about it?"

"Where do you hurt?"

"All over."

"What an answer. You're not getting the help you need because you're not being specific enough. What particular part of your body is screaming at you right now to do something about it?"

"My left hip really hurts when I try to walk even a short distance."

"Your body is yelling at you to do something about this pain. Did you tell the doctor your hip was killing you?"

"Yes, but he just passes it off as not important."

"Has he taken x-rays of your hip?"

"No. He says he can find nothing wrong."

"My dear, I would suggest you find yourself some other doctor who will listen when you talk."

"But they don't listen. They always act as if I don't have all my marbles and am only wasting their time. Besides, a hip can't cause this overall pain."

"Yes, it can. You evidently are pampering the left side of your body, instead of standing straight when you walk. This throws everything out of alignment, so naturally your whole body hurts."

"What good sense you make, dear Annaliz. How about being my doctor? You have all the answers."

"I don't know all the answers. All I use is common sense. Go back to your doctor and insist you have an X-ray. If he won't do it, find someone who will. By the way, did you call me up to ask about your illness?"

"Oh, dear, I almost forgot what I called about. I have this dear friend, Alejandro, who wants to fix up a place for his great granddaughter. He says it's really run down, and needs a person with knowledge of how to remodel a house to bring it back to its former beauty. He's seen John's place and loves it. He's set on having you do it."

"I haven't worked that way, Ramona. As you know, I buy a house, live in it until it's finished, then I sell it and look for another one. I've never worked for anyone else. I don't know if I'd like it."

"Please," her friend said. "Just talk to him. He's been bugging me to introduce you. May I at least give him your phone number? It won't hurt to talk, will it?"

Alejandro called and persuaded Annaliz she should see the house he was talking about, before she made up her mind.

"If you don't want to do it after you've seen it, then I'll understand but, please, just take a look."

The house was a hacienda, on a ranch, at the edge of the city. The yard was overgrown with weeds at least five feet high and the fountain, which had once been beautiful, needed a complete overhaul.

The outside of the house looked sturdy enough. The arches forming the arcade in front were only slightly cracked. Annaliz thought they would be easy to repair.

The entrance had two old, interestingly carved, mahogany doors. Those could be saved.

She walked through the rooms as if in a dream. The dining room was huge and beyond was a ballroom big enough for a commercial dance hall. There were six bedrooms along one side of the house.

Annaliz marveled at what she was seeing. This place must have been built in the 1780's. Over two hundred years ago.

Murals of Mexico covered one wall of the ballroom and, along the hall, were beautiful tile paintings framed in gold leaf.

The beams, a foot wide, thick with years of cobwebs, had not sagged. Here and there, covered with cloth, were big forms that could be furniture.

She asked Alejandro to lift the fabric on one piece and found, to her delight, a dining room table large enough to seat twelve. Insects had eaten some of the legs away and the table leaned at a dangerous angle. When she insisted the table be protected from any more damage Alejandro brought some boards from the yard, and together they propped it up.

"The top looks in good shape. New legs can be matched to the old ones. It can be restored."

He raised his eyebrows. "You are intrigued? No?"

"Yes. I am. But I've never done a restoration before and that's what's needed here."

"What is the first thing to do?" he asked.

She grinned as she brushed cobwebs from her hair. "A couple of maids would be nice, to clean the place up but, " she added, "someone must be here with them, so when they lift the coverings from a piece of furniture, it will be known whether or not it can be saved. Many people discard things because they think a leg can't be repaired."

"Good. Exactly what I want you to do. I knew you could remodel this to make a lovely home."

"This will not be a remodel," she said. "It will be a restoration. We will make no changes in the rooms except to repaint, repair, and bring its life back as much as we can."

She stopped. "What am I saying? This is no job for me. It needs someone experienced in working with antiques. The museum might have someone qualified; if not the one in Mazatlan, perhaps in Mexico City. This is way beyond my expertise."

Alejandro smiled. "John says nothing is beyond your expertise."

"He probably has no idea of the age of this house or he wouldn't say it. I'm guessing it is over two hundred years old and will be fabulous with a little attention."

"It's one o'clock," Alejandro said. "Why don't we go to lunch and discuss this problem? I'm sure, if you don't wish to do it, you can help me find someone who will be adequate."

"Okay. We can discuss it, but you won't want someone merely adequate. You need someone who loves antiques. Someone who knows their history and is willing to make certain the things put in the house, to refurnish it, are suitable for the period."

At lunch Alejandro said, "Have I made a mistake in thinking I could fix the house up so my great grand- daughter would like it? She is not an antique, this girl. She is very modern. She may not want to live in a two-hundred year old house."

"What does she do, this modern woman?"

"She's an artist. You may have heard of her. Angela Renoza?"

"But of course I've heard of her. All of Mexico has heard of her. Her paintings are fabulous."

"They are very modern, you know. She does not paint old houses."

"I know, Alejandro. She's a surrealist." Annaliz smiled. "Any artist

177

will love this house, once it's restored, surrealist or not. Artists love beauty and this will be a beauty."

"But only if you oversee the work, and please call me Alex. I can tell. You are wishing you could do it. Couldn't you read up on antiques and find enough material to do it for me?"

"I wish I could but I know my own limitations."

"John says you have no limitations."

She grinned at him. "He's a fool. He likes the house he bought from me, so he thinks I can do no wrong, but believe me, with this house I could be very wrong."

Smiling at him she said, "No, Alex, I want to. I really do want to, with all my heart, but I won't do it. It's a special place and should be restored by a museum because it will be a showcase. None of my houses were showcases, only homes."

"Will you come see it when the museum person is through?"

"Of course. I would want to."

"And if there are any finishing touches you could add, you would do it, wouldn't you?"

"Certainly, but I can't imagine the museum leaving anything undone."

She smiled, thinking of how beautiful the house would be and said, "There is one thing I would love to do. I'd like to fill the rooms with bowls of cut flowers. I can just visualize it. This house was meant for people who love each other."

"It was built by my great, great grandfather, Antonio Jesus Maria Sanchez Villa." He laughed. "They gave so many names in previous days. He and his wife lived there for over fifty years. I believe it was a love match."

"Many marriages were not. I understand parents decided who was to marry in those days."

"See. You know more about those days than you think you do."

She patted his hand. "Come on. I know what you're trying to do and it won't work. I am not going to do it."

"Could we at least be friends? I would like to see you again."

"Of course. I never turn down a chance to have a new friend."

She added, "and I am interested in the house and will follow your progress with interest."

In the following days Alex called often. He kept asking her to work out with him.

First he wanted her to join his aerobics class. When she told him she did not exercise, he couldn't believe her. "At least you could walk with me in the morning."

"How far do you walk?" she asked.

"About five miles."

She roared. "Alex, if I tried to walk more than a couple of blocks you would have to carry me home. I was not meant for exercise. Stop trying to make me do it."

"But you are in such good shape. I was sure you must work out in some way."

She said. "I dance and when I remodeled houses I only directed. I did none of the work myself."

Laughing, she said, "I'm lazy, Alex. Face it. I prefer to do only what is absolutely necessary. I do not want to exert myself."

"Yes, I know. You know your limitations. Well, I am older than you, but I don't let it slow me down. I am 90. What do you think of that?"

Annaliz gasped. "It's not possible."

"How old did you think I was?"

"About 75. You have a young body. You can't be 90."

He yelled joyfully, "Hey, you noticed my young body? That gives me hope for the future."

"What kind of hope?" There was laughter in her voice.

"What do you think?"

"Dream on." She reached to hang up the phone, and chuckled as she said, "I'm looking for a younger man. You old guys can't keep up with me."

12

John had been gone for over two months when, in his usual evening phone call, he said he was home, and would be for a few weeks. He said, "The editors have asked me to do a lot of rewrites this time. It seems I wrote the book too rapidly, so there are a lot of details I left out. They want them included."

"Do you have the same editors as last time?" Annaliz asked. "I always thought the woman with the funny name was really helpful. What was she called?"

"You mean Karlinda? I'm sorry to say she got a better job, with a larger publisher, so I'm working with new people. They do seem to know their jobs so I don't expect any big problems. How about dinner? I need to go where I can really talk to you."

They chose a quiet corner on the terrace at the Playa, because most of the other restaurants played loud music and it was difficult to talk.

"I wrote this book so quickly, it was as though I couldn't type fast enough," he said as they ate their salad. "The words to say were there, in my brain, waiting to come out. It was as though someone were dictating to me. Every day, new ideas were there, without me even having to think about them. Have you ever felt that way, writing poetry?"

"Yes, I have. Not too often, but when it happens, it's as though God is giving me directions. It's great."

"It's better than sex." He laughed

She laughed with him. "I guess you haven't had any for awhile."

"Why do you think I came home? I thought you might need it. I'm younger than you, you know."

"Oh, I know all right. You're continually telling me."

He grinned at her. "You enjoy arguing with me as much as I enjoy trying to come up with something to make you mad. You know I don't really want to hurt your feelings. I think both of us enjoy a good contest."

He continued, "If I hadn't made you mad you wouldn't have made me mad and I might never have begun to write this second book."

She looked at him and laughed. "Hey, if it helps, I'll be glad to make you mad any time."

Laughing with her, he said, "I hope next time I'll be able to make you really mad. It might give me a block-buster."

He then sighed and shook his head. "I can't believe it. My editor says this book will outsell *King's X*."

"I figured it had to be going well. You seem so relaxed."

"I need to go back to New York in a month. It's soon, I know, but I begged

185

my publisher to let me come home for a few weeks and unwind."

He added with a grin. "I told him if I didn't get home soon, someone else would take my woman."

She smiled back at him and said, as she had so many times before. "I am not your woman but if it got you a few weeks here with me, I can't complain. I've missed you."

She looked at his hair, which was whiter than she remembered and thought, time is creeping up on both of us. I am so happy to have him as a friend. I hope he's not working too hard. I don't want anything to happen to him.

John sighed. "It's good to be home with you. I hope I can relax a little bit. It seems I've been on a writing high for the past six months or so."

"Six months is a very short time to write a book."

"I know. It probably will never happen again. My editor told me so when I wanted to show him the first drafts. He said no one could write a book in that short a time. I think he thought it would be lousy but, as soon as he read the first few chapters, he told me he was hooked. He said, 'If I'm hooked, John, then the readers are going to be too. We have another best-seller on our hands.' I wanted to get on my knees and thank God. It has been a long, dry spell."

Teasing, she said, "And what will your next book be about, Mr. Lambert? We are all anxious to know."

"Ok. Ok." He had to laugh. "I don't panic any more when they ask me. I can tell them the basic plot of this one. I know I don't have to go any farther."

He shook his head sadly. "It was just when the pages in my computer were blank, my mind went blank when someone asked what I was writing. You kept telling me the feeling would go away eventually, but it never did."

"You evidently didn't want it to go away."

"I know. I've thought of that too. My body was probably telling me 'You don't really want to do the work a new book would entail.' My body was right of course. It is a hell of a lot of work."

"But it was worth it, wasn't it?"

"Yes, now that I know it's going to be a best-seller. My problem was, I didn't believe in myself."

"And do you think it will be easier next time?"

He laughed and made as though to slap her. "For God's sake let's not go that route. At this moment I don't even want to think about it."

"So, what do they have planned for you when you go back? I'm sure you'll start the circuit again. It seems you are always on a continual round of talk shows."

He grinned boyishly. "I suppose it will come in time, but first I'm going to meet Julia Roberts, the movie star. She's thinking of using the two books combined to make a movie. The price they're thinking of paying is staggering."

Annaliz looked at him with a knowing grin. "You're not as interested in the money or the movie as you are in meeting Julia. I can tell."

He said a bit self-consciously, "I'm expected to meet certain people. The price of fame, you know."

"Aw, fame. Once you've had it you can't help feeling hungry to have it again. Be careful, John. You know, perhaps better than most, fame comes and goes. You can be a hero one minute and in the next you are a nobody."

She sighed. "Fame comes fast and goes even faster and, when it's gone, the feeling in your stomach is so hollow you know you'll never be full again."

"You sound as though you've been there."

"At one time I was. When my book of poems was published I was on cloud nine. When it only sold 2000 copies and the publisher no longer wanted it, I was hollow for awhile, just as I said."

She shook her head. "It was a sad time. I was afraid I was no good at what I felt I did best."

"Is that why you didn't write another? I love your poetry. You should do another book."

"No, John, I finally made up my mind I didn't want to ever have to live with that feeling again. It was not worth the time and effort."

"But you didn't turn to drink, as I did?"

She smiled, remembering. "I was lucky. I found a new man and he filled my life with love and laughter."

"A new man, huh? By the way, how are you and Alex getting along?"

"Hey, is that a question? Did you think I needed a new man? Is that why you sent him in my direction?"

"No. No. He's a great guy. I thought you'd enjoy working with him, remodeling his house."

"Have you talked with him lately?"

"No. As you know, I've been in New York."

"The house he wanted me to work on is over 200 years old. It has to be restored, not remodeled. It needs someone from a museum, not me."

"But you've been doing it for over 30 years. I was sure you'd know how to fix whatever he needed."

"Yes. I've been doing it for a long time but I've always done remodels, not restorations. This is going to be an absolutely gorgeous home when it's finished, but it can't be done by me. I know when to step aside and, for this house, I really need to."

She added. "When I did remodels I could do everything the way I wanted. With a restoration everything has to be put back the way it was originally."

She sighed. "I don't feel up to doing anything new, especially something with a great deal of research and work and I'd be doing it for Alex, not for me. I don't think I would like having someone else in on the decisions."

She looked at him and shook her head. "No. Don't send me any jobs, John. I've been there, done that."

He said with concern in his voice. "You're tired."

"Now don't start," she said. "I'm feeling fine. Can't a girl slow down now and then without being accused of being old?"

"I didn't say it. You know I wouldn't."

Quickly changing the subject, she said, "By the way, you haven't told me the name of the new book."

"I got the name from the first one. Since that one talked about Kings, I thought this one should tell the Queen's story. It is titled, *Queen's Exes*. As you told me to do, I wrote it about women like you. Actually it still tells men's stories, but from the standpoint of how women have influenced them."

She leaned forward and in a low voice, as sexy as she could make it, she asked, "And how do I influence men, kind sir?"

He reached out to pat her arm and said, "Just by being you, my dear. All you have to do is say what is necessary for your welfare and I will walk over broken glass to get it for you."

"Oh, John. You know I was only kidding."

"Well, I'm not. I mean it. I love you. Will you marry me?"

She looked at him and smiled. "The answer is no, as usual, but you knew before you asked. Why you keep asking I'll never know. Now tell me, is this book as sexy as the first one?"

"Sure. You can't write any other way today. Sex sells."

Queen's Exes did outsell *King's X.* It went to the top of the New York Times' best-seller list in three weeks and was chosen by the Book of the Month Club.

Talk of a movie with Julia Roberts went on and on. John met her and wrote he wasn't impressed. He said she didn't look anywhere near as glamorous in person as she did in the movies. Annaliz wasn't sure if it was true or he was only being kind.

He went on tour and was gone for months at a time but kept in touch, sending her long letters and calling on the phone. She could follow his progress this way and, although it wasn't the same as being with him, she knew he was thinking of her.

She kept busy with volunteer work, teaching her poetry class and going to the Friday dinners. It was late summer and the sun was very hot during the day, which made the sunsets spectacular.

Maria got married and there was a lot of merry-making for about a week before her wedding.

There was a party for her and all the Friday-night friends were invited. Being women, they laughed until they cried about the strange and funny things that happened to them just before they got married.

Annaliz worried a bit about Maria. She didn't seem to be enjoying the evening. She wasn't her usual happy self, not the way a bride should be.

Is she worrying she made a mistake in planning to marry Henrico? Her parents don't like him, I know. He isn't as fun loving as she is but people do say opposites attract. I hope everything turns out all right for her.

The church was filled with Maria's friends and family and she looked beautiful, as all brides do. Her dress was one her grandmother had worn over 60 years before, embroidered in white roses across the bodice and around the hem. Annaliz wondered how much they had to let it out in the back to fit Maria, who was not in the least slender.

The reception was in the Freeman hotel and went on for hours. The Freeman had been closed for years and had reopened only last month. Annaliz thought, this must be a feather in the cap of her parents, to be the first to use this beautiful room for a wedding.

The ballroom was decorated in Maria's favorite color, yellow. Roses at every table gave a rich look and their heavy scent filled the air. Annaliz was delighted with this. Many roses, she thought, have no scent at all. It was wonderful to sit between dances and smell their wonderful aroma.

She enjoyed herself, because her friends were there, the champagne was dry, the food was good and the mariachi music was delightful. After dancing several dances with Pedro, Miguel, and other friends, she finally called it quits at midnight and went home in a taxi. She wished John had been there but, as usual, he was on television, appearing with another talk-show host.

When she kissed Maria goodbye she said, "I know you're moving to Arizona but please keep in touch. We are all going to miss you. Do call or write me. You're one of my favorite people."

13

At last the unthinkable happened. She fell. It was in the hospital corridor, near the children's wing. A toy was left where it never should have been and Annaliz didn't see it in time. She put out her arms to save her face and hit the floor with her knee. She also turned and bruised an ankle. "Why does a knee always hit first?" she muttered as people helped her up.

She was well known at the hospital and Doctor Alvarez insisted she stay there, to recuperate.

"I can go home," she argued. "My knee hurts a bit but otherwise it's only a sore ankle."

"Try to walk on it," the doctor said.

Just one step and she knew she was in trouble. The pain was so intense it brought tears to her eyes. The nurse helped her back to a chair.

Why, oh, why, didn't I watch where I was going? I've walked these corridors as a volunteer every week for the past two years. Why did I have to get so careless?

"You see," The doctor said. "You must not go home until you can walk without pain. I do not think anything is broken but we will read the x-rays and see."

He turned to the nurse and said, with a smile. "Tie her to the bed if you have to. I don't want her leaving here on her own."

Annaliz said, "Never fear. It hurts too much. Couldn't you give me some morphine, or something, to kill the pain?"

"Or something is what we will give you," he said. "We do not hand out morphine like aspirin. It can be habit-forming, you know."

She tried to laugh. "Hey, doc, how long does it take to become addicted? Do you think I'll live long enough to need a fix every day?"

He frowned, not amused. "I believe in giving as few drugs as possible. If you can stand the pain it would be well to take nothing stronger than aspirin."

"And how long is this pain going to last?" She wanted to hear him say she could go home the next morning but he was evasive.

"A bruise can take longer to heal than a sprain. I don't want you to go until you can stand on your own."

"That could take days."

"Yes, it could." He grinned at her. "The hospital is picking up the tab, in case you're thinking of expense. We take care of our own, especially since you fell on our premises."

She grinned back at him. "You think I might sue, huh?"

'No. I don't think that. The hospital values your services a great deal. I want you up and around as soon as possible." He left with a wave, saying he would be back in the morning.

Sun came through the window. Annaliz could look out to the street. The hospital was in an older part of town, and here she could see shops lined up, each with only about 20 feet of frontage. A taco stand was squeezed between a car wash and a copying shop. A tire company had old tires stacked high. None of the storefronts had been painted in a long time. Signs were painted on them, however. Some advertised the different businesses and some were beer ads. All you could say for them was, they were colorful.

Some people would say this is a slum, she thought, but it is my town, a town I love, where the men and women smile at me as I walk along the street. No one pays attention to the way the outside looks. If they want to look at

201

something prettier they know they can go to the Golden Zone.

Sighing, she knew now what the next day would bring. She had given the hospital her daughters' names when she first came to work as a volunteer. Next-of-kin's names were required in case someone became really ill. She had meant for the hospital to call her daughters only when she had a fatal illness, not for such a happening as this and she wished there were some way she could keep them from letting the girls know what had happened.

I sure don't want Karen to come and begin demanding I move back to the States. I can't stand her hovering. "I hate hover," she murmured, but there was no one to hear her. The nurse had already made her bed and left.

Lying on the bed she remembered when she was fourteen and had sprained an ankle. What a difference the years can make. I didn't even go to bed then. The doctor put on an ace bandage, gave me a crutch, and said, "Stay off of it as much as you can for the next three or four days."

Now here I am, at 78, having to stay in a hospital for God knows how long for just a bruise. It doesn't even hurt unless I'm standing up. What kind of a sissy have I become? Yeah, I know. It takes longer for things to heal when one gets older, but this is ridiculous.

Tiffany arrived the following afternoon.

"Karen couldn't come," she said. "She promised to teach a drawing class to some first graders this weekend."

"I'm delighted to see you," Annaliz said. "You don't hover."

"Whatever that means." Tiffany said.

"It means exactly what it sounds like. Karen stands over me demanding I give up and come home. When I say 'no' she says, 'Show me you can walk on your own and I'll stop talking about it' and of course, right now I can't do it and she will…"

Tiffany was laughing. "I can just see her doing it too.

Now tell me. Is it bad? Will they have to amputate?"

"Quit making fun of your mother. Of course, they won't amputate. It's only a bruised knee and ankle, but it does hurt like hell and they won't give me anything but aspirin to take away the pain."

"How long will you have to stay in the hospital?"

"They won't tell me. They say the x-rays show no broken bones, so it has to be just a bruise. I never knew a 'just a' to hurt so bad."

They both looked up as Alex walked in. "What are you doing in bed?" he asked with a frown. "Get up this minute."

"How did you know I was here?"

"You should know, in a small town like Mazatlan, news like this gets around fast."

"Maz is not a small town. How did you hear about it?"

"I met Soriana for lunch and she told me."

Annaliz looked at him sternly. "So. You are now dating nurses? I know Soriana. She's very pretty."

"Sorry," he said. "You're letting your romantic soul lead you astray again. She's a cousin."

"Yeah." She grinned at him. "I know you have dozens of cousins. How come all of them are pretty?"

He grinned back. "It must run in the family."

A commotion at the door made them turn. John walked in, a suitcase in his hand. "I came as fast as I could."

He dropped the suitcase, came to the bedside, gave her a kiss and said, "My dear, how are you?"

"What in the world are you doing here? You're supposed to be in New York."

"I was in New York until Ramona called to say you were in hospital. What is wrong?"

He looked around at Tiffany, Alex and the nurse and asked, "Is it a wake we're holding?"

"Oh, for heaven's sake, John." Annaliz said. "It's only a bruised ankle. Ramona shouldn't have called you. I don't know why everyone has decided I'm at death's door. Quit hovering. You know I hate that."

The nurse said sternly, in Spanish, "All of you clear out and let the poor woman rest. This is too much excitement for her."

Alex, the only one who understood all of the nurse's words, howled with glee and said, "The nurse thinks we're to much for Annaliz."

He said to the nurse. "Forget it. This lady lives on excitement. If she didn't have some, at least every other day, she wouldn't be happy. We are helping her get better. Laughter is the best medicine, isn't that what is said?"

The nurse looked at Annaliz and asked, "Do you need another pain killer?"

Annaliz took a moment and then said, "Strange. A few minutes ago I was really hurting. Now it's gone."

She looked at the faces of her daughter and beloved friends and knew it wasn't excitement that kept her going. It was the love in their eyes, the kindness and caring she knew was hers, without having to ask. Before she could stop them, tears filled her eyes.

"Now see what we've done," John said. "She is hurting. We must go, but we'll be back tonight."

When they were gone she berated herself for showing tears. I'm not in that much pain. Damn. When friends are kind I get maudlin. I suppose it comes with the dotage every one talks about. I will not give into that.

But you cried, she reminded herself. Okay, so I cried, but it's not self-pity. It's not. I don't allow myself to feel that.

The nurse came back in a few minutes with a walker. She said, "The doctor thought you ought to try this. He felt you might be able to go home sooner if you could walk by yourself."

"I'm not ready for a wheel chair yet. Take it away."

"This is not a wheel chair. You told Doctor Alvarez you wanted to go home and he's trying to help you. A couple of days of practice with this will help you walk better and it will make the bruise heal faster. You can't stand on your leg now but it needs to get blood down to it to get better. Tomorrow you will get up and use this."

"I will not. I can't stand up yet. It hurts too much."

"You are a sissy." The nurse said. "Little kids, hurting worse than you, do it every day."

The hospital stay went by quickly. Her room was full of flowers and laughter as friends came and went, bringing good cheer and color into the drab room. John was there every day, sitting close, holding her hand when there were no other visitors.

Home again, after 5 days in the hospital, made Annaliz look around with wonder. Aurilia had been in to clean. Everything was spotless. The flowers she had received, while at the hospital, were everywhere. Outside, the camellia was in bud and the orange tree, which she planted at every house she remodeled, was filled with blooms and fruit.

All this beauty makes me feel young again. I'm still hobbling around with this darn walker, of course, but I feel today I could move mountains.

Maybe it's just because I'm home. This house invigorates me.

Tiffany had gone home on the third day and her sister had arrived to take her place and "see Mom safely home", as she put it. Daughters could be helpful, Annaliz finally admitted. Even Karen was friendly.

Does a simple bruise make such a difference to them, she wondered? They've not given me this much attention before. She chuckled. Maybe I should have been ill more often.

She was sitting quietly in the garden, reading, when Karen came out of the house and blurted out, "Remember my picture that was in the gallery?"

"Yes." Of course she remembered. Who could forget it?

"I burned it."

Annaliz said quietly. "I'm glad."

Karen looked at her in surprise. "Then you knew what I was trying to say?"

"Of course. Anyone who saw it knew you were in a rage when you painted it."

"I didn't know it myself, at the time." Karen said. "I wanted to show Edgar I could paint. He didn't think I could."

"And is it important to you now, now you can't show it to him?" Annaliz wished she could pull her words back but Karen did not flinch. Instead, she looked her mother square in the face and said, "I've come to terms with my life, Mom. I've forgiven Edgar and myself for the kind of marriage I had. I was competitive and so was he. I could never get the best of him and it made me angry. I know now most of my misery I brought on myself. I've been thinking of the past a lot lately."

She looked away. "Do you have a lot of regrets about your past, Mom?"

"No, my dear. I don't think about it. I think it's morbid to dwell on things long gone. I can't change anything that happened then. I look to the future."

Karen looked back at her in surprise. "Mom, I hate being blunt, but how much of a future is there for you? You're almost 80." She frowned. "I know you think you can go on forever, but the end will come. Shouldn't you be getting ready for it?"

Just like Karen, Annaliz thought. She says she doesn't want to be blunt but she knows no other way to operate. She asks questions of people no one else would let themselves ask and she thinks she is doing them a favor by being real. The girl does not know the meaning of compassion.

Annaliz waited a few more minutes, thinking about her response and then said, "I think I'm ready. I'm not going to go one minute sooner than I have to but I recall, in the book, *Aztec*, a man said, '*I came out of my mother's womb and began my dying*'. I've often thought how appropriate that sentence is."

She said slowly, "We all know birth is the beginning and we also know the end is waiting for us somewhere, some time, from the day we're born. I've learned patience since I've been in Mexico. What will be will be. I'm not afraid to die. All I hope is, the next phase will be as interesting for me as this one has been."

"What a strange thing to say. Aren't you worried you might not go to Heaven?"

Annaliz said, "I've never worried about going to Heaven. I think we make our own Heaven and Hell right here on earth. Right now, in this house, I am in Heaven." She added, "I think death is just one more phase we all must go through."

"I don't think I really understand death but," Karen said, "I may finally be growing as you told me to do. I remember thinking, just the other day, after hearing a song by Gordon Lightfoot. He sings, '*If you plan to face tomorrow, do it now*' and I think he's right. I plan to stand up and face what comes, every day from now on."

Annaliz watched her daughter march back to the kitchen and thought, I hope she can, but she is so set in her ways I'm afraid she'll keep re-acting instead of acting. I don't think she's ever had a thought in her head someone else hasn't suggested first.

They had asked Alex and John to come have a drink with them before they went to dinner. Walking around the room, exclaiming over each new item Annaliz had acquired since his last visit, Alex picked up the Mayan head and said, "Could my ancestor, who built the house, have looked like this?"

"I hope not," Karen said. "I've always thought this to be the head of a very cruel man. Look at his mouth, stern and unsmiling."

"Cruel, perhaps, as leaders have to be, but I like his eyes. Look at those laugh lines. You don't get those by never having any fun in your life. Annaliz, how did you come to buy it?"

"I thought it very beautiful."

"Beautiful?" A chorus of disbelief from them all.

"Yes, the sculptor must have loved this man. It may have been his father or his leader but he knew the man intimately. I feel it deeply. If you have no love for someone, I do not think it possible to carve something so completely human as the artist has made this man out to be. Look at him. Really look. I know, if I walked into a room where he was standing, I would know him instantly."

Alex said pensively, "I can see what you mean. I hope he was my great, great, grandfather. He has character, and a bit of grandeur, I think. He would have fit in my house."

14

A few days later, driving by the house Alejandro wanted to restore, Annaliz saw his car and went in. "Hey, Alex. How's it coming?"

She could see nothing had been done with the exception of the cobwebs, which had been removed.

"Annaliz. I was just thinking of you. Nothing has been done, as you can see."

"Wasn't the museum able to help you?"

"A man I know came from the museum, took one look and said he would charge $500,000 pesos to do the job. I told him I'd think about it."

"I told you it would be expensive."

"Yes, but this guy wanted me to pay him. I wanted the museum to do it as a project. I felt it would mean more to Angela if it were done by a museum, as you suggested. I knew the furnishings would probably cost a lot but I didn't think the museum would charge such a terrific fee."

"Have you talked to the curator himself?"

"Why do that? I know Alfonso. He goes to my church. He's a Christian. He wouldn't overcharge me, would he?"

"Agnostics are not the only ones who overcharge, Alex. I have known so-called-religious people, who are just as greedy as the next fellow."

"Will you go with me to see the curator then? I feel out of my element. If it's going to cost a million pesos or more to restore it, I may have to find Angela another house."

"Why has it been empty all these years? Surely something so beautiful would not be left like this."

Alex smiled. "Legend says it has a ghost. My great, great grandmother is supposed to come on rainy nights and dance the flamenco in the ballroom. When I was a kid and it rained I brought my friends and we would wait for her to show up but she never put in an appearance."

He shrugged. "Because of the story no one wants to rent it or even stay in it overnight. I thought if it were restored and people could see how beautiful it was it would give the place enough glamour so someone would like living in it. I know a ghost wouldn't faze Angela. She'd probably love the idea."

Annaliz said, " I'll gladly go with you to see the curator. I want to find out what he'll say. I'm sure he'll be thrilled."

The curator was a woman, Teresa Santos, a tall blonde, dressed in a dark blue business suit, as her office required. Annaliz was not surprised to see the suit. Women in a business or profession in Mexico had to wear them to show the world they were business people. Protocol demanded it.

Senora Santos welcomed them and, after they told her of their project, she said, "I am interested. If the house is truly over two hundred years old, I would like to see it. If it could be restored, could it be seen by the public?"

Alex said, "I'm giving it to my great granddaughter. If she says it can be shown, I would be happy to have the public see it. My ancestor built it. I am very proud of it."

Teresa made an appointment to see the house the next morning. By the time she walked through the rooms and examined the furniture where it lay worm-eaten, she said the house would be a marvelous project for them.

"We have many interns at the museum. How wonderful for them to have the experience of working with something this old. We have many houses in Mazatlan a hundred years old but nothing like this. Why didn't the museum know of this one?"

Alex said, "This was one of the original haciendas in Mazatlan. At the time it was built, it was a ranch, many miles out of town. The city has grown around it and since it has a very high wall, it's been overlooked."

Hesitantly he asked, "Do you have any idea how much it will cost to restore the whole thing, furniture and all?"

"I couldn't give you an estimate," she said, "but the interns work for nothing, of course, so you will have their labor free. The work to restore the house itself looks minimal. It is the furniture that will cost. Finding people who can carve the way they used to will be difficult and probably expensive."

She added, "But of course, we will ask permission before anything is done. If you feel something is too expensive we can, perhaps, choose a different craftsman."

Knowing Alex always wanted the best, Annaliz knew he would never object, no matter the cost.

As the days went by, she went to the house often. The interns cleaned the walls, ceilings and floors. The old tile showed wear in some places but after much discussion they decided not to try to replace it.

When she asked why not, one of the interns said sternly, "Most of the beauty in this house is because it was built by craftsmen who knew their job. Anything looking new will undermine everything we are trying to do. No. I know this old style will be impossible to match. We must, and I certainly want to, use it as it is."

The hunt for carvers began. Annaliz was pleased by the museum's search for carvers who could copy old work. They came from all over the country; some from Guadalajara; some from Tlaquepaque, and some from as far away as Chiapas. She knew Alex and the curator were interviewing many young men, eager to try their hand at whatever was needed, even if they hadn't done it before. Some said they could copy anything. Some, more honest, admitted it would be difficult. She could see why. The tools used years before were no longer available. The right tools would have to be made before any carving could be done.

The men who suggested finding old tools were listened to, and sent to museums around Mexico to sketch the equipment needed, to make copies for the use of today's craftsmen. Annaliz felt it would take six months to finish the restoration.

As she looked at the beauty unfolding in the house, she thought of the many houses she had remodeled. Some of them were run down, not as much as this, but I tried to keep whatever had character. Mostly I wanted a house to be comfortable for a normal person to enjoy and I think they were. I always had a plan to work from. She smiled, remembering the one she remodeled that John bought. The yard was so huge I wasn't sure I could find enough plants to make it look like a garden, but by adding the pool I made it work. He loves the goldfish I put in. He keeps adding fish until one day he'll need a larger pool.

Alex' house is going to be a museum. It would be a shame to keep it for just one family. It will have to be open to the public some of the time.

I believe Angela, knowing beautiful things when she sees them, will understand the need to have it on display and not want to keep it to herself.

15

Late in February Annaliz was driving to town. She needed shampoo, and the only place carrying her brand was a pharmacy, six miles away. She never minded having to drive so far on the sea-wall road because she could see the beautiful, deep blue ocean.

As she turned the corner, onto the main thoroughfare, a policeman with his hand in the air stopped her car. Ahead she could see a group of children with band instruments.

Oh, I forgot. It's almost time for Carnaval. These kids must be practicing their parading. Many streets will be closed off for the next month, as everyone gets ready for the fun to begin.

So that was the music I heard yesterday afternoon. The children in the school near the house must have been practicing.

As she waited for the band to pass, she remembered the first time she had attended Carnaval.

I had no idea what to expect. I assumed it would be like celebrations at home, where the bands played, parades took place on a Saturday, there were a few minutes of fireworks, and then everyone went home and waited for the next year's excitement.

Carnaval doesn't happen that way in Mazatlan. It's the 3rd largest pre-lenten festival—only Rio and New Orleans are bigger and people flock from all over the world to participate in the event.

So many arrive for Mardi Gras, called Carnaval in Mexico, the hotels and RV parks are full. If you want to stay, you have to make a reservation months in advance. I was glad I had come almost a year before and had a hotel room.

I knew the fun began on Thursday before Ash Wednesday, and continued through Fat Tuesday. I couldn't believe a day would be called that! Ramona explained to me everyone ate all they could on Tuesday because, for the next 40 days, they would be on a fast.

Parades happened every day, some in the morning, some at noon and then the Grand Parade, with the Queen of the Carnival riding high on the prettiest float, started at one o'clock on Sunday and lasted until almost four.

I remember the floats were huge and flower-decked, with a band on just about every one so there was continual music, even when the school bands were not playing.

It was interesting to see how different these floats were from the kind seen at the Rose Bowl festival. Those had to be covered in fresh flowers. In Mazatlan, paper flowers were the favorites. Four hours went by so fast I couldn't believe it was over.

I was staying at the La Siesta Hotel and the bombardment, or fireworks as I called it, took place on Saturday night, out in the bay and on the beach directly in front of the hotel.

The bombardment commemorates the time Mazatlan was attacked from the sea. None of the locals I talked to knew what war it was but they knew the French had been attacking, and they knew the French had not won. They thought this all the more reason to enjoy the fireworks.

My room was in the back, so I couldn't watch from a balcony. I went out into the street, in the afternoon, to join the crowd. Booths were doing a good business.

People ate tacos hot from the makeshift stoves vendors used for the day. Ceviche was a favorite dish, as it's eaten cold and could be placed on top of a crisp tortilla and carried on a napkin so it didn't drip. I bought one of those and it was delicious.

Many women were selling eggshells full of confetti. They didn't have booths but squatted on the curb and sold their wares. These women saved their eggshells for a year and when Carnaval came around they colored them, filled them with confetti and taped them closed.

It was a tradition to walk down the street, breaking the shells on the heads of everyone you met and getting pelted yourself. I couldn't believe how much confetti I got on my clothes. My bedroom floor was covered with it the next morning. Laughter was the order of the day.

Since then, the celebration has become more sophisticated and eggshells are no longer available. I miss them, Annaliz thought. They added much fun and laughter to the occasion.

Coca cola was in great demand, as was beer in tall-necked bottles.

Annaliz remembered, if she had ever wanted to buy a souvenir of the

Mazatlan Carnaval this was the place and time to purchase it. There were key chains, money clips, ashtrays, hats with the city's logo, and almost anything one could think of, that they might want to buy.

I could tell Carnaval was not totally a Mexican party, for I heard voices from Germany, the US, France and England. I felt the excitement beginning to build inside me just from brushing up against so many different people, all intent on one thing: having fun.

I went back to the restaurant for dinner with Pancho and we could not believe the hustle and bustle of so many people having dinner at only seven in the evening. Most Mexicans dined at eight or later. That night it was as if they had so much to do, out in the street, they wanted to get dinner over with early.

The street in front of the restaurant, and many streets on the parade route, had been blocked off and people of all ages were walking, buying eggshells full of confetti, eating whatever was on sale, laughing all the while.

The excitement in the eyes of the children and their parents filled me with exuberance. I had never felt that elated before. It is a feeling I still get during Carnaval. There is something about having my world full of joy that sets me off.

The city of Mazatlan goes all out for Carnaval. There are parades, queens chosen for everything from The Best Disco Dancer to the Prettiest Girl In Town. There are bull fights, baseball games and, of course, soccer tournaments.

Although Pancho and I didn't usually have much to drink, we were in the Carnaval spirit that evening and we each had a Margarita. We both ordered shrimp, deep-fat-fried in garlic butter, and laughed when we thought of how we would have to be careful not to breathe on anyone.

We then went out into the streets to join the festivities. We each bought half a dozen packets of eggs and went happily breaking the shells on the heads of everyone we passed. Our heads and shoulders were soon showered with the colorful paper There was so much confetti spilled this way, the streets were about four inches deep in the stuff in the morning.

Bands played at each intersection and some mariachi bands came strolling along, playing as they went. For a bottle of beer for each member of the band, they would be willing to play a special song for us.

The fireworks, although I use that word knowing it doesn't fit the type of ammunition set off at this event, were bright, huge blossoms of brilliant color in the sky and each blast was so loud it made us jump. We could feel the ground move under our feet.

This can't be fireworks, I thought. This is a true bombardment. They must be using bombs. It's almost like a real battle.

The bombs continued for about thirty to forty minutes. When the last, beautiful one had exploded in the sky everyone clapped and began to wend their way back to the center of the city to catch a bus for home.

I asked Pancho if there was anything else we could do.

It was almost midnight but I knew I was so stimulated I would be unable to sleep. He suggested we take a ride out to the end of the bus line, sit on the beach and watch the stars.

"It will help us unwind after all the excitement," he said.

We had taken buses to the end of the line before, so he could show me various parts of the city, and I was delighted at the idea. When we sat on the beach, the stars seemed so close, I felt I could reach up and touch them. So far out of town there were only a few hotels so no lights interfered with our view of the stars.

It was especially nice in the bus. Mothers and fathers carried their kids, who were sleepy after all the day's activities and the love the parents had for their children showed in the loving way they cuddled them.

The kids, who were not yet sleepy, were fidgety, wanting to run up and down the aisles of the bus and yell at the top of their lungs. I was still excited and felt like doing it too but knew adults didn't behave that way.

Mothers in Mexico do not chastise their children for this kind of deportment, as probably would happen in the States. They think a child needs to run off his energy, so they let him do it as long as he is not hurting himself or others. How much easier on the parents and the children, Annaliz thought.

That night the bus emptied bit by bit until there was only Pancho and me, three families with wide-awake children, and one young woman.

She sat at the back of the bus, hands folded in her lap, over a packet of confetti-filled eggshells. She was dressed in well-cut, expensive clothes. The cost of the white, angora sweater she wore, would have fed the Mexican families in the bus for a month.

She didn't smile at the children's antics. I felt sorry for her for, several times when I glanced back, I thought she looked sad and lonely.

Pancho must have thought so too, for he suddenly took a few eggs, from the full sack he carried, and stood up.

He went along the aisle, cracking eggshells on the heads of the delighted kids, until he reached her side. His hands were empty by this time and he made a motion as if to ask her if she would share her eggshells.

At first she just looked up at him with a frown and then looked down at the eggs in her lap then, wearily, as though she had the world on her shoulders and nothing mattered to her any more, she passed the packet up to him.

Pancho slowly and carefully opened the sack and took out one egg. She watched him lift it high and her eyes widened as she saw what he planned to do.

I saw her mouth open and knew she was saying, "Oooh" as she watched the confetti shower her white sweater with pink and purple color.

The glorious smile she gave Pancho said to me that all evening she had hoped this would happen to her. It had not, and she thought she was going back to her hotel to spend another night, alone and unloved.

The woman stood up, pushed Pancho aside with a wide gesture, and went down the aisle, bopping the rest of her eggshells onto the children's heads, laughing all the while.

I know it was without thinking, the parents in the bus began clapping. The kids, thinking this was some new fun, began clapping too. I was crying too hard to clap.

This was Pancho as I knew him to be, aware of other people, their joys and their problems. Sharing his love for everyone, able to understand another's pain and help them get through it. It was no wonder I loved him.

That was an awesome moment. I guess I can say, like the young kids, "That night we were all on a high."

Carnaval does that to me. I love Carnaval. I can't wait for it to start again.

So engrossed in her memories was Annaliz, she was surprised to hear horns honking and see a policeman waving her on.

Good heavens. How long have I been sitting here? The band of children had scattered into the surrounding streets. She, and the cars she was holding up behind her, were the only things not moving on.

She put the car in gear and sped away, making herself a promise once again to call the La Siesta hotel on the street of the bombardment. She rented a room there every year, on the Saturday night of the Carnaval.

When she became tired of all the festivities she could go to her room and still watch the fireworks from the balcony.

When someone asked why she did this, she said, "Don't you get tired walking around for hours during the celebration? I have my fun down on the street and then I can go to the hotel room to rest and still see everything. I think it's the smart thing to do."

Her friends, the ones who had known her longest, knew enough not to ask her if she tired easily because she was getting old. She would have denied it vehemently.

16

After the fire was over, Annaliz couldn't tell anyone exactly how it happened. She knew she was frying chicken; had a pan half full of grease, and had already put in one piece, when flames began shooting up the back wall.

She told John. "I've no idea how long I stood there in astonishment. I finally went for the fire extinguisher. I had a hard time getting it free from its buckle and when I tried to turn it on I could see it wouldn't be any use. The cupboards were on fire. I guess I panicked." Sadly she said, "I kept running from room to room wondering what I should remove and in the end removing nothing. When the firemen came I was standing there in a dirty dress and bare feet. I didn't even have my purse."

"Oh, darling," John said, "What a horrible thing for you to go through. I don't know how you managed."

She shook her head. "If I hadn't had such good friends here it would have been a lot harder. I didn't worry about the bare feet. After all, this is a resort town and people go around like that all the time, but the dirty dress bothered me. I asked the fire chief to find me a cab and I went to the Playa."

"The hotel would have been the last place I'd think of. It's kind of posh, isn't it?"

"Yes, but I know Jose, the bartender, and knew he would help me."

She chuckled. "I gathered up my dignity, walked straight to the bar and told Jose I needed him."

"If I'd been here you wouldn't have had to go through all that. Why didn't you call Ramona?"

"She was out of town, visiting her son in Austin."

"You know," she was thinking out loud, "The house is completely destroyed inside, all my mementos of years past are gone, the place probably can't be restored because the smell of wet smoke clings, even to adobe and brick. I know I've been careless many times. This has taught me a good lesson."

John said, "When Jose called to say your house burned down, I almost died until he said you were okay. My God, if anything had happened to you I don't know what I would have done."

"He was a big help. He called you, got the name of your gardener, who had a key to your house; had a maid bring me a clean dress." She laughed. "He said he was sorry he could do nothing about the shoes."

John said, "I'm glad my house was here for you to come to. I should have given you a key a long time ago."

He added angrily, "If I hadn't been in the middle of the damn tour I could have gotten here earlier."

"For Heaven's sake. I was well taken care of."

"But I want to be the one to take care of you." He smiled. "Now, since your house is gone, you can stay here with me."

She looked around at the heavy wood furniture John had installed when she moved out. It's just not my style, she thought. Even if it were, I don't think I'd ever want to live here again. I loved the house that burned. I don't have energy enough to remodel another one from scratch, but I definitely don't want to live with anybody. Not even John."

She said, "Oh. No. I don't want to do that."

"Why not?" He grinned at her. "We're compatible. You've said so yourself."

She smiled back at him to take some of the sting from her words,

241

"Compatible is great for once or twice a week but not for an everyday thing. I need my privacy."

"I'll give you privacy. I'll even build on a separate wing, if it will help."

"But it wouldn't help. This is your place, not mine. It's your house, your yard, your flowers, your things scattered around…"

"Well, dammit. Scatter your own things around and then it would be our things, not just my things."

Annaliz sighed. "I don't think any man can understand what I'm trying to say. I need a spot for me. Not yours, not ours, but mine. Something I can look at and know it's my private space. If I want to keep people out, I can. If I want to invite them in, I can. I decide, not someone else."

"You could do it here. I wouldn't interfere."

"But you see, I would wonder how you'd feel if I invited someone new. I'd have to ask your permission. After all, if a house is ours, it means it's yours too. No. I can't live that way, John. I'll look for another house to remodel."

"Every one in town will think we've had a fight."

She sighed. "Come on. If you're going to worry about what the neighbors think, what am I doing here at all?"

"They know we're going to marry sometime."

"Then they're mistaken. I do not intend to marry, ever again."

"My Lord, Liz, you've been divorced for over 30 years. Was he such a terrible husband you believe every other man would be like that? What did he do to you, anyway? You've never said and I've never asked. Now I would really like to know."

She walked away and with her back to him she said, "He could charm the birds out of the trees when he wanted to. He kissed ass any time he was with a person who had more power than he did.

For those he thought were beneath him, he stepped on hard."

A sob caught in her throat before she could continue.

She said, "He never laid a finger on me but there are times, even now, when I wake in the middle of the night and can feel my bones crunching."

John cried out, "But, darling, I never mistreat you, do I?"

"No." She turned back to him. "You're not a husband. You're a lover. There's a world of difference in those two words."

With a sigh, she continued. "When a man signs the marriage certificate, he believes he owns the woman and can do as he pleases with her. The lover knows he can't be sure she'll always want him."

Vehemently she added, "I will never be owned by anyone again."

"I've always known you were a free spirit, Liz. I wouldn't try to tie you down."

"You don't think you would but you've not talked about your marriage. Was your wife treated as an equal or as just an appendage, taken care of for the sake of the children?"

"I tried to treat her well. She never complained."

"Who would she complain to? No woman wants to admit her marriage is a disaster. Were you happy with her?"

"Yes. I think so, for the first few years anyway. I became a problem for her when I began to write and needed space. I think she resented that."

He said hesitantly, "I've never said this to anyone before but I think, when she died suddenly of a heart attack, for a moment, just for a moment, I was relieved I wouldn't have to battle her for space anymore." He sighed. "I felt bad about it for years."

"Don't you see?" Annaliz said. "I'm doing the same thing right now. I'm battling for space of my own and you resent it. You think I should do what you want me to do."

Tears came unbidden. "Please, John. I don't want to lose you as a lover, but I won't accept you as a husband. If you want us to go on as we have been, I think it would be wonderful but if not…"

He yelled at her, "Do you mean this is the end? Do you think you can just say goodbye?"

His voice softened and he said, "Oh, God, Liz, you need me right now but I need you all the time. Don't leave me." He reached out for her and she went into his arms willingly.

"I do love you," she said. "I hope you understand why I don't want to marry."

"All I know is; I want you to be happy. I'll help you look for another place."

She had forgotten how maddening house-hunting could be. It had been over two years since she'd remodeled one.

This time she hoped to find something already built, with a nice patio.

"And, of course, an orange tree," John kidded her.

"I can always add it," she said. "But I do need a good-sized yard. I need open space more than space in the house. The things these real estate people keep showing me are American houses in Mexican neighborhoods. Little ticky-tacky things I wouldn't be seen dead in; an ugly California copy. They have no yard at all."

She went on. "I can't understand how people can come to Mexico to live and insist on having the same house, the same furniture and the same ideas they had at home. Why bother to come to a foreign country if you bring the US with you?"

Annaliz sighed. "Do you know I've had salesmen who want me to rent a condo. They keep saying it has a swimming pool. They can have their damn pools. I don't want to be cooped up in one of those high-rise buildings. I would die."

John looked at her with a grin. "You can always stay with me. I have a huge patio. It even has an orange tree."

"How about letting me buy your house and you go live in an apartment?"

He laughed. "Could I come visit?"

"Depends on whether or not you behaved yourself."

"For that I just raised the price another hundred thousand. You can't afford it."

"Too true. Anyway, I have a thing about not wanting to live in a house I once enjoyed. Going back would not be the same. Your smell would be all over it."

"Hey. I don't smell."

"You know what I mean. The ambience changes once someone else has been in it awhile. I don't think I could ever get the same feeling back."

"Houses give you feelings?"

"Oh, yes. They talk to me. They say 'Color must be added here.' Or 'This spot is perfect for your poetry writing.' They even tell me which way the bed should face."

"What the hell does that mean? Where it faces doesn't matter."

"Maybe not to you but it does to me. I want it to face east so I can face the sunrise."

John roared. "You've never been awake to see the sun rise as long as I've known you. Who are you kidding? Next, you'll be telling me you're taking yoga lessons."

"What's wrong with yoga?" she demanded.

"Oh, my God. You're not?"

"It's none of your business if I want to exercise a little."

"Too bad Alex isn't here. He'd be delighted. Who talked you into this?"

"No one did. Gustavo, next door, suggested it might be good for me when I said one day my knee was aching."

"Who the hell is Gustavo?"

"You've met him. He was my next door neighbor."

"You mean the little skinny guy with acne? How could you listen to him?"

"He said at one time he was very fat and yoga helped him lose weight."

"You don't have to lose weight. You've always been thin. I like you just the way you are. Why didn't you tell me your knee was aching? How long has this been going on?"

He stopped talking for a moment, then said, "I see.

This knee only aches when a man tells you he goes to yoga classes. By damn. You're flirting with him. You're leading him on. Well, I'll fix him. I'll tell him you're my woman and he's to stay away."

She sighed. "There you go again. I am not your woman. Anyway, he's taking boxing lessons. He'd probably beat you to a pulp."

"So." He sighed. "I can see you've been thinking of the possibility we might fight. Well, I'm sure he'd take one look at my manly physique and run. Now, " he said seriously, "Does your knee really bother you or were you just saying it to get his attention?"

"Ever since I fell at the hospital it has kicked up now and then. It really is nothing to worry about."

"We dance a lot. Does it pain you then?"

"Sometimes, but I just ignore it. I like dancing."

"Be honest with me," he said. "How many other aches and pains do you have you never mention? I know you must have some. We are both getting old..."

He stopped when he saw the look on her face.

"I asked you never to use that word."

"Oh, hell, Liz, are you ever going to face up to facts? Do you think you

251

can go on ignoring what looks back at you every morning in the mirror? I love you just as you are. I don't care what the calendar says. Why should you?"

"I don't care what it says either, but I don't like you reminding me of things I don't want to think about and, "anyway, I don't look in the mirror."

"How do you comb your hair? How do you put on lipstick?"

She grinned. "I've been doing it so long I can do it by feel alone."

"You're impossible," he said. "Come on. Let's go look at the next house you won't like."

It took them several weeks but they finally found the right one. It had a huge patio, three bedrooms and a kitchen, then an area useable as a living and dining room.

Looking around, John couldn't see it as anything but a house full of problems. Annaliz could see the possibilities.

She told him to go out in the patio. She was going to stay in one of the bedrooms for awhile.

"I suppose the house is waiting to talk to you."

"Yes. It is. Now go away and let it happen."

As he went out the door he called back, "Don't forget to tell it the bed must face east."

It took four months to finish the place but Annaliz moved in during the second month of remodeling.

When John asked why she didn't stay with him where it was clean and comfortable until she was through decorating, she said, "The maids have finished scrubbing the place down. I have a bed, a kitchen and a bath. I don't need any thing more for the time being."

She added, "I want to be there when they're doing the painting. I've chosen a very soft, light green and I can never be sure it's going on right unless I'm there."

'But you go there every day."

"I know, but it's not the same. I need to live there."

Although the house was hidden from the street by a stone wall, Annaliz decided the exterior must be painted yellow, a color loved by her Mexican friends.

At home, in the Northwest, I would probably choose white with something bright for trim. Here it is expected one would choose a color as bright as possible for the whole outside. Perhaps Mexicans like bright colors because there is so much greenery around them. They need the contrast.

When Annaliz invited her friends to come for an open house, they were delighted to see what she accomplished.

"It's a dream home," Estrella said. "I wish I could move in. I'd love to sleep in the bedroom with the east window."

Others remarked the gardener had done a fabulous job in the patio.

Ramona said, "I don't see an orange tree. Haven't they gotten around to planting it yet?"

Annaliz said, "I'm not having one this time."

Everyone looked up in surprise. "You've had one at every other house. Why not this one?"

Even John was amazed.

"When the house burned, I decided it was the end of an era for me. Whatever I did from then on would be new and different. I'd have a new outlook on life."

She looked around at each of them. "I decided I would have a different type of house and, as you can see, this one is a little larger than any of the others. I plan to give a lot of parties and I'm going to do other things. I'll take a few classes at the University. I want to be a totally new person, now I have the opportunity."

"But you loved orange trees."

"Yes, I did. But I've decided to change. I have arranged for the gardener to plant a Jacaranda instead. Within a year or two it will be giving me shade and I like shade. Also, when it blooms it's gorgeous. I'm planting it close to the outside breakfast nook so its blossoms will blend with the pale blue I have on the chairs."

No one thought this strange. Annaliz was known for doing such crazy things.

The guests had brought gifts for the housewarming. There were bouquets of flowers, perfumed candles, bottles of wine and when Annaliz opened the box from John, she found a Mayan sculpture.

"This guy," John said, "is not as mean looking as the one you had but I was sure you'd like another one."

"It's perfect."

I hadn't wanted to bring any memories from my other house. It's like John to think all things must remain the same. Change is not in him.

I like change. I think it builds character and Heaven knows I could use some. It's taking every ounce of my strength to live through this evening. I thought I could handle it but now I wish I'd waited another week before showing the house.

The remodeling has taken a lot out of me but I'm trying hard not to let it show. My plans didn't include being this tired. Even though I would never say this to some one else, sometimes I have to admit to myself I'm old; I know the only thing I have left is just the need to carry on; to keep pretending. I'm afraid if I ever let down my guard it will be the end.

When everyone except John had gone home, and they were sitting quietly, holding hands, John said, "You were right. This house must have talked to you. It's talking to me now, saying, 'See. This is the way I was meant to be. I was only waiting for the right person to come along and love me.' You were the right person."

"John. That's very poetic."

"I never knew poetry, or love, until I met you. I was like the house. I needed to have the right person come along to love me. Someone who would listen to me and teach me to listen to her as well. You have taught me many things, Liz. Perhaps the most important is, we must leave each other alone to live our lives as we want to."

He went on. "I wish I'd known that before I met you but I didn't. There were many times when I thought I was teaching someone the error of his ways when, actually, all I was doing was trying to change him into my image. I've been an egotistical fool."

"We all are fools, John, if we think we can teach any one else anything. No. Each of us must learn what is necessary in our lives in our own way. You are an observer of life. You know each of us needs to be ourselves in order to keep growing. You wouldn't be a great novelist if you couldn't see that."

"You know, darling." John said thoughtfully. "I think I could now write a book worth reading."

Annaliz grinned at him. "Let's not go too far, John.

No one would buy a book worth reading. You said yourself sex sells. You had better keep on writing that kind."

"Do you mean you like sexy stories?"

She pulled him to his feet. "No. I don't much care for second-hand love. I like the real thing."

17

Tiffany appeared one afternoon, without warning. She marched into the house, put her hands on her hips and said,

"Did you know Henry has been unfaithful for five years?"

Annaliz looked up in surprise. "What a strange thing to ask. How would I know? I haven't been there."

Tiffany's lower lip trembled. "Everybody in town knew except me. They've been talking about it for years."

"How do you know?"

"One of my so-called friends knew and didn't tell me until I caught on." She wailed the next sentences. " She said she was sure I knew and didn't care. How could anyone think I could be so uncaring?"

"And you're sure it's true?"

Tears were running freely down Tiffany's face. "He said he was going bowling. Said his team was playing in a tournament. I've never gone before, but this time I thought it might be fun to watch."

Now she was in a fury. "He wasn't there. One man said Henry hadn't played in a tournament for years. I couldn't believe it. When he came home I asked him how the team came out. 'Did you bowl well?' I asked. He said, 'I got a 220. Pretty good for me.' I shook my fist at him and yelled, 'Did the woman you were with think you bowled a 220?' He didn't even have the decency to deny it."

Annaliz asked, "Did he say who it was? The woman, I mean."

"Oh, yes. He bragged about it. It's Brianna. She's 33 years old, the daughter of a friend of mine. You'd think he'd won the Nobel Prize, he was so pleased."

"Did you kick him out?"

"I tried, but he wouldn't go. He told me this had nothing to do with me. It was just a 55 year old having some fun. He said Brianna wasn't the first and she wouldn't be the last. I didn't know what to do, so I came to you. You went through it, Mom. Karen says you ran away. That's what I want to do. Please, tell me how."

"First, I want you to wash your face and put on the prettiest dress you brought with you. We'll go out to dinner. It will give both of us a chance…"

Before she could finish Tiffany said, "I don't feel like going anywhere. And I didn't bring anything pretty. I wasn't in a pretty mood."

Annaliz said, "I want you to look your best tonight. That green thing I bought you, the one you left here last winter will do. You said you'd leave it here, for it was too risqué to wear in Cameron."

"It's too risqué, even for Mexico, Mom. It's nothing but straps."

"Well, I believe in being risqué when it's needed and right now it's needed. Go put it on."

When Tiffany came out ready to go, Annaliz admitted, even to herself, the dress was certainly nothing but a wisp of fabric with 'all straps', but I think a woman needs to feel she is beautiful at a time like this.

The dress hangs perfectly on Tiffany's willowy figure. The green makes her look like a wood nymph.

As they walked into the elegant restaurant at The Inn At Mazatlan, heads turned. Tiffany lifted her chin and straightened her shoulders.

Annaliz thought, it takes courage to come out at a time like this, when she's hurting so badly, but the admiration she's receiving from the men, and even women in the room, will more than make up for the effort.

I'm glad I made her come. She is stunning in that dress. No matter what Henry may do to her in the future, she has had this moment, and she will remember. It will help her cope.

In bed at night she wondered why Tiffany came to her, instead of one of her friends. I suppose, because she knows I'm 78, she thinks I'm wise.

I wish I could tell her wisdom doesn't necessarily come with the territory. I don't know if I've even learned much from the mistakes I've made, and I've made plenty.

I stayed longer with my husband than I should have, thinking it would be better for the children. I still don't know if it was the right thing to do but I was really happy when Karen eloped early and Tiffany finally got married. It gave me the freedom to leave the marriage I had wanted to leave for a long time.

I talk to other women who are going through the same thing I did and they too, say, "I don't know if I should stay or go." It's a difficult decision.

The next morning Tiffany said, "I've decided to go back home, Mom. I know people will be snickering behind my back but I can take it. I've done nothing wrong. I can live with myself but," she added, "I won't live with Henry. I'll get a divorce and he can fend for himself. He has no idea how much a wife does for a man."

She grinned. "A mistress may be great in bed but what about feeding him, doing the washing and making his dental and doctor's appointments? No. I think he'll have it hard." She continued. "I'm sure he'll be pleading with me in a very short time and I'm going to enjoy telling him to forget it."

Annaliz said. "Just be sure to get a good woman lawyer. I know, from experience, they can be the toughest. Be sure Henry plays fair with you financially."

"He's not the type to play fair. I should know how he is. He'll consider, since he was the one making the money, he should now keep it all."

"Tiffany." Her mother's voice held concern. "A divorce may be the most traumatic thing you'll have to face in your lifetime. Words are said that should never be uttered. A divorce is a very cruel thing. It's not something to go into lightly."

In a serious voice she continued, "It's somewhat like deciding to get married. At times you'll be happy and sure your way is the right way and then, in the next moment, you'll be sure you're wrong to even contemplate it."

She took a long, drawn out breath. "You'll spend your days singing, but believe me, there will be many nights of crying."

With awe in her voice, Tiffany said, "Did you go through all that?"

"Oh, yes. And more."

"Mom. I've often wondered why you didn't get married after your divorce. Was that the reason - you didn't want to be hurt again?"

"Partly, and partly because I found companionship with a man didn't have to lead to commitment."

Tiffany gasped. "You mean you had affairs?"

"Why are you surprised? You didn't expect me to live celibate all my life, did you?"

Tiffany giggled. "It's just because…" She was laughing and couldn't finish her sentence.

Annaliz tried not to laugh. "After all these years, you still can't imagine your parents having sex. Well, it happens in the best of families."

"Sorry, Mom. I can't help it. I know you're fond of John and Alex. Do you go to bed with them, or shouldn't I ask?" She began giggling again.

Annaliz sighed. "I suppose what you want to know is if a woman of 78 is still interested in sex. Yes. I am."

Thoughtfully she said, "An orgasm now can be even more powerful than it was at 18. I have always believed, that at least one orgasm a week keeps a woman healthy."

She grinned at Tiffany. "I'm going to say no more on that subject."

Her daughter said "Mom, I had no idea you were having such fun. Maybe I should move down here too."

"Get your divorce first and then we can talk about it."

In the next few months the girls, as she called them, came to see her more often. They confided in her. They asked her opinion, which they had not done previously.

For some reason she had grown in their estimation but she didn't know why.

Could it be, since they both were now unmarried, one divorced and one a widow, they could place her in a new category, one they now shared?

I can see Tiffany having an affair but I don't think Karen will ever take that road. Somehow, even if she hadn't loved him, and she may have, she would probably feel it would be unfair to Edgar. Also the neighbors would talk.

Has the alienation of years past been because they can't understand what I went through with my divorce? Have they subconsciously hated me for going away?

Well, no use worrying about the past. It's over. I'm just glad we get along so well now.

Karen was happy teaching painting techniques to children and Tiffany had given up writing poetry and was now into designing clothes.

"She's made a couple of things for me," Karen said. "They're real knockouts. You should have her design something for you, Mom."

Annaliz shook her head "I can't see me in a knockout. No. Mother Hubbards were designed a long time ago."

"You don't wear those things. You still have a good figure," Tiffany said. "I can see you in a shiny sheath with a mandarin collar. You would look stunning."

"I'd need the collar all right. This scrawny neck of mine shouldn't be seen. But one thing you may not think of is my hands. They tell my story, they and my wrinkles. There is only so much one can do with clothes. If you want to design something for me, make it simple, in a soft shade of green, perhaps, but I don't want any part of it to call attention to my years."

She put her hand up to her face. "I'm not ashamed of them, you understand. I've earned all the wrinkles but I'd rather people noticed my smile and not my, shall I call them, my infirmities?"

"Mom. Don't run yourself down. You really look good. All you need is a face-lift."

"It would take a ten ton truck to lift this face."

"I'm thinking of doing it," Karen said. "Many of my older friends have had it done."

"You're young enough to get away with it. I've seen some of your older friends after a face-lift. They look like a death's head: just skin stretched tight over bones. No thanks. That's not for me."

Tiffany said, "Mom, you are always so sure about what is right for you. How do you do it?"

"By trial and error, my dear. Lord knows I've had time to experience just about everything at least once."

The girls leaned forward in their chairs. They think I'm going to tell them some dirt about my past. Well, they can just keep on thinking. I've watched older people tell of their past and I knew they were telling lies. It was in the wry quirk of their mouth, where they were almost ready to laugh, or it was in their eyes, which said, "If you believe this, I could sell you the Brooklyn Bridge." We all, me included, love to exaggerate. I refuse to go there.

Annaliz said, "I don't care to talk of my short-comings. Let's discuss something else."

Karen said, "Lately I've been thinking about the risk you took, coming down to Mazatlan on your own, not knowing a soul. Weren't you frightened?"

"Scared out of my skin."

"Why didn't you come home?"

"After I had proclaimed my freedom? Don't be silly. I knew there would be snickers behind my back then. I was stuck here."

"What did you do?"

"I became an interpreter for a real estate agency.

I wasn't supposed to work. Americans couldn't unless they had emigrant status, which I didn't want at that time. The company paid me under the table."

"Did you ever wish you could go back to the States?"

"In the first few months, of course. I cried myself to sleep many a night, missing my children and my friends. Then, I began to make new friends. I enjoyed my work. I was no longer afraid."

Tiffany giggled. "I suppose you had your first affair then."

Karen said, "What are you talking about? Mom doesn't have affairs - or does Tiff know something I don't know?"

She looked over to where Tiffany was convulsed with laughter and demanded, "I want to know. You said affairs. Do you mean she's had more than one?"

Annaliz tried to calm her down. "Karen, be sensible. You're a widow. Haven't the men come on to you? That's how it was for me."

She had to giggle. "They were hard to resist at times but I had other plans."

"Mom, the men who came on to me, as you call it, were my best friend's husbands. They kept telling me I must be lonesome and they could do something about it. It was horrible. They made me hate all men."

"I know. That was one of the reasons I fled to Mexico. The feeling will pass eventually. You'll find someone to love who loves you and those memories will fade away."

"There's no love in an affair,' Karen stated.

"Maybe not the kind of forever-love you're thinking of, but there is friendship and respect…"

"No. There is no respect."

"How do you know if you haven't tried…? Oh," she said, "I see. You did try it and it was horrible. I'm so sorry."

Karen began to cry. "I hate men. He was like some kind of animal. There was no love, no respect."

She wailed, "How can you say an affair is something one should do?"

"I didn't say it was something everyone should do. However, if you find a friend and both of you are willing to go to bed together, I find nothing wrong with it. It can be another way of saying 'I care about you. I want you to be happy.' It's not for everyone, of course. Before I came to Mazatlan I wouldn't have dreamed of it happening to me."

"So," Tiffany asked. "How did you have enough nerve to have an affair down here?"

Annaliz grinned impishly at the girls. "I met a good looking, fast talking, real estate salesman."

Tiffany pleaded. "Tell us about it."

275

"No way.   Go have your own affairs.   I'm keeping my memories to myself."

18

Driving home from a luncheon with her poetry class, Annaliz began to feel the familiar tingle in her legs and the fullness in her head.

She pulled off on the side of the street, shut down the motor and waited for the feeling to pass, as it had done several times before.

Now, at least if I keel over in the car I won't have an accident, she thought.

She tried to look at the cars passing by, but her vision was blurred. It felt as though her eyes were crossed. This bothered her more than the tingle in her legs, because this had never happened in previous episodes, as she called them.

Trying to be sensible about the whole thing and not panic, she leaned back against the seat and closed her eyes.

This is the worst one I've had. Is this the end for me? Am I going to die on a public street?

She had to smile, as she thought of how horrified Karen would be. Poor girl. I don't know how she ended up so worried about appearances. Tiffany is not the same way. She can laugh off most things, but not Karen. If someone doesn't conform, they are beyond the pale in her book.

I know she has my best interests at heart but I wish she would take time to have more fun. It must be hard on a person to be continually looking for something to worry about.

Annaliz had been half dozing, not paying attention to the street, when there came a tap on the car window. A policeman was standing there wanting to talk to her.

She rolled down the window and he said, "You can't park here. See that sign? It says 'No parking'. I'll have to give you a ticket."

Knowing many policemen in Mazatlan hated writing tickets and would rather be paid cash to go away and leave you alone, she got out her wallet. The smallest thing she had was a fifty-peso note. She tried to hand it to him.

When he didn't take it right away she thought, Darn. He really is going to give me a ticket. Now I'll have to go to court.

Instead of taking the money, he said, "Let me see your papers."

When she handed the papers to him, he opened them and indicated she should put the money inside them.

He knows what he's doing is illegal. He doesn't want anyone to see him accepting a bribe, Annaliz realized.

He deftly palmed the note and returned the papers. "Move on," he said.

If he had been someone, anyone else, she would have tried to explain she was feeling unwell, but she looked at his uniform that had not been pressed and how it couldn't hide his huge stomach and knew it would be useless.

This was definitely not a cop with any pride, not one who cared about the citizens of his city. This one was on the take and didn't care about helping anyone else.

Carefully she put the car in gear and pulled out into the street. It's only about half a mile home. I think I can make it that far. Things in my head are beginning to feel better. She pulled into the garage, shut the door and turned off the motor.

She kept telling herself she was only a few feet from the kitchen and only a few feet further to her bedroom but somehow she couldn't get up enough energy to move.

She wasn't sure how long she'd been sitting in the car, when somewhere, far away, she heard the doorbell. She tried to yell but nothing came.

Unable to open the car door or call out and, not thinking of anything else she could do, she had to let it ring.

Over and over she heard the bell and then a voice from the kitchen yelled, "Annaliz, where are you?"

She felt, even if she could yell, it wouldn't be loud enough to be heard, but she was thinking a little more clearly so she hit the car horn. The kitchen door flew open and there was John, looking bewildered.

"What are you doing out here?"

He turned on the garage light, took one look at Annaliz, opened the car door, picked her up and carried her to her bedroom. Covering her with a blanket he picked up the phone.

In a weak voice she said, "I don't need a doctor."

"No," he said. "What you need is a hospital."

"No. Please, John, I'll be all right. Just let me rest for a few minutes. This will go away if I have just a few minutes to let it pass."

He hung up the phone and looked at her with a frown. "This has happened before, hasn't it?"

"Yes, but it's nothing. It will be over in a little while. It comes and goes and it usually lasts only an hour."

"Why haven't you told me?"

She tried to smile. "I know what a worry-wart you can be. I didn't want to give you something else to worry about."

He sat on the edge of the bed and took her hand. "Darling, I want to have the privilege of worrying about you. Please don't keep something as important as this from me. Tell me about it. What happens? How does it make you feel?"

"It's nothing, John. Just a tingling in my legs and a fullness in my head. It goes away if I sit or lie still for a bit."

"Could it be a stroke?"

"No. I don't think so," Annaliz said. "I understand a stroke paralyzes one side of the body and I've noticed nothing like that. I must have done too much today. Sometimes it comes when I've been too active."

"It could be small strokes," John said. "I've read about those. I've heard strokes can be caused by little veins in one's head breaking and forming tiny blood clots. In most cases it seems to dissipate without doing any damage; that is, in most cases. How will you know if it will?" He frowned. "Shouldn't you see a doctor and find out once and for all what is happening to you? I'd feel better if you knew for sure what's causing this."

"I've read up on this kind of thing, John, and it seems nothing can be done to stop it. Usually the doctor gives a person with these symptoms a blood thinner. I'm already taking one. I started taking an aspirin a day quite a few years ago."

"But maybe that's not enough."

She tried to sit up. When he tried to make her lie down Annaliz pushed his hand away and said, "I told you it only took a few minutes for it to go away. I'm feeling fine now."

"Are you sure? You look kind of pale."

Swinging her feet over the side of the bed she stood up and before John could grab her, dropped back onto the bed, unconscious.

She woke to the sound of men's voices, feeling the IV in her arm, realizing she must be in a hospital. She turned her head to look around the room and saw John standing beside the bed, talking to a doctor.

She said, "What happened?"

John came to her side, knelt down and said, "Darling. I'm so glad you're awake. We've been worried about you."

"How long have I been here?"

"The ambulance brought you in last night about nine. It's now ten o'clock in the morning."

Annaliz looked at the dark circles under John's eyes and said, "Oh, John. You haven't had any sleep."

"Don't worry about me. The doctor says it was a good thing I called the ambulance when I did. They started giving you a blood thinner right away and it may have dissolved the clot that caused you to faint."

She looked at the doctor. "Did I have a stroke?"

Dr Alvarez frowned at her. "John says you've been having these episodes for quite some time. Why haven't you been in to see me?"

"They never lasted for more than an hour before. I felt I would be okay if I just rested until it was over."

She looked at the doctor accusingly. "You didn't answer my question. Did I have a stroke?"

"Yes," he said. "It was a small stroke but it was a stroke. You are fortunate it wasn't worse than it was. I need to make some tests to see if you have any impairment from this but, knowing you, you're going to deny there is anything wrong."

He folded his arms across his chest and said, "Young lady, the next time you have one of these strokes it could kill you."

She moved her arms and legs and found they worked all right under the covers. My eyes don't feel crossed any more. My limbs work all right. What else do I need to check on? Everything seems to be in the right places.

She looked at the doctor, started to rise from the bed, and said, "I'm okay now. Can I go home?"

Dr. Alvarez laughed. "I knew that was the first thing you'd say. No. I want you to stay a couple of days so I can, as I said, do some tests. If it looks as though we might be able to handle this with medication alone, then you can go home."

"However," he said, "I will want someone with you for the next week, to monitor the medication. I know how you hate pills and I want to be sure you take whatever I prescribe."

He looked at John. "Can you do that for her?"

"Of course. I'd be happy to stay with her."

"Oh, for heaven's sake. I'm not a baby. I can take a few pills if I know I have to."

John grinned. "When it's doctor's orders that I stay with you, do you think I'm going to pass up this opportunity?"

"How about your publisher? I thought you were supposed to be in New York on Thursday."

"I'll just call him and tell him something more important has come up. He'll understand."

Annaliz had to admit that for the first few days it was nice and cozy having someone around to talk to, someone who knew her well enough to give her some space now and then. It wasn't so nice when John monitored her pill input, telling her, hour after hour, it was time.

After the third day Annaliz said to John, "Do you think I'm now capable of taking my own pills? Do you think I still need a keeper?"

"No, of course you don't need a keeper. You want to send me home, don't you?" He put his arms around her. "But I like being here with you. Can't I stay forever?"

She gave him a hug. "You've been a big help, but now I need to be by myself. You need to go to New York anyway. Your public is waiting."

"Okay, I'll go, but promise me you'll take your pills every day, when you need to."

When he had been gone for a week Annaliz realized one morning she had forgotten to take the pills for the last two days.

Am I getting forgetful or is my body telling me I've taken enough of these things? John said take them when I need to. I feel fine without them. I certainly do not want to take pills the rest of my life.

I'll cut down to one every other day and if I still feel all right, then I can cut down to one or two a week. I've been able to handle all my ailments that way, up to now, and I don't see why I can't go on doing it. Doctors don't know everything.

She laughed at the thought she might live to be 120. I will certainly have outlived the doctors who say I can go any time. They'll probably be dead before I am.

Being sure she knew how to handle her problems, she went on doing the usual chores around the house, cooking her own meals and attending the Friday night dinners with her friends.

I'm glad John didn't tell them I was in the hospital, she thought. They would be concerned. They wouldn't hover but I would see the anxious looks on their faces each time they said hello.

I know they wondered why John was staying with me. She giggled. They probably thought he was moving in.

I know he would like to, but I value my time alone. I look at some of my women friends, with husbands, and watch how they have to be at home at a certain time; and how they have to make three meals a day. I don't know how they stand it. I would hate to go back to cooking for someone else.

She grinned. If I want to have cornflakes for supper, I can. I don't think any husband would sit still for that.

"Hmm," she said aloud. "Cornflakes sounds good to me. I think I'll have some right now."

She went inside and as she reached for a bowl, the phone rang. It was Estrella. "My men have all left me to go to a baseball game," she said. "I hate eating alone. How about meeting me somewhere to watch the sunset?"

Annaliz said, "You caught me just in time. I was about to have supper."

"Oh, what are you having? Maybe I can come and share."

"How about a bowl of cornflakes?" Annaliz asked.

In a horrified tone, Estrella said, "You're not having that for supper. Good heavens, have you forgotten how to cook?"

"No," Annaliz said, "but if I'm hungry and want to eat in a hurry I just reach for the box."

"Pedro and the boys would never go for that." Estrella said. "they want beans and tortillas, hot off the grill."

Annaliz laughed. "Now you see why I'm not married."

Her friend protested, "But don't you get lonely? I would die if I had no men around and had to eat cornflakes for supper."

291

"Well, I don't have to have it," Annaliz said. "In fact I would be delighted to go to dinner with you. Where did you have in mind?"

Estrella said, "Last week Pedro and a friend took me to a funny little spot on the beach, in front of the El Cima hotel. It's just a palapa and doesn't look very pretty but the ceviche was wonderful."

"Hey," Annaliz said. "I love ceviche. Let's go."

19

A few weeks later, when John made his usual evening call from New York, he asked how she was feeling.

When she said she was doing fine, he asked if she could come stay for a few days. "If you really are okay, that is. Have you been back to see the doctor? What did he say?"

"Oh, John. I don't need the doctor. I haven't had an episode since the one I had when you were here."

She giggled. "You must be in trouble or you wouldn't need me."

"It's not me in trouble," he said. "It's Alex. I don't know what to do. I need your help."

"What in the world is wrong?"

"Can't tell you over the phone. You must come. I can't handle this by myself."

Annaliz arrived in New York, anxious about Alex. John met her at the plane and before he could say a word, she said, "Tell me. Is he ill? What is it?"

"I'll tell you at the hotel," he said.

Although she kept asking, during the long taxi ride to downtown New York, he refused to say anything but, "It's not fatal, but I can't cope with it. You'll hear all about it once you're settled at the hotel."

She wondered, as they pulled into the drive in front of the Waldorf Astoria, if John stayed there each time he came to New York, or if he only did it when she was with him.

He's not flamboyant, she thought, as they walked into the beautifully appointed room. He must plan nice things like this just for me.

He made her wait until she had unpacked and was seated comfortably in a chair, then he said, "Alex is getting married."

Annaliz said indignantly, "And you called me all the way up here, and made me think he was dying, just to tell me he's getting married?"

"For heaven's sake, Liz. We have to talk him out of it. He's infatuated with this woman and won't listen to reason."

"John, you know we never interfere in another's life. We don't have the right to tell anyone else how to live. How could you think that? Why would Alex want to hear reason? Let him have his fun. He can afford it. If he feels like getting married at 90, let him."

John's eyebrows went up. "He's not 90. No way. He's younger than I am."

"He may look that way because he exercises and you don't, but he told me himself he was 90 and I believe him."

"But that makes it even worse. He probably won't outlive this woman and she'll inherit his fortune."

"What if she does? Alex has been married three times. He moves at such a fast pace, she'll have to struggle to keep up with him. She will have earned every penny. What age is this woman anyway?"

"I haven't seen her but the way he talks about her she must be a 30 year old. He raves about the way she can keep up with him when he runs…"

Annaliz interrupted. "I can see why it would be important to him. He wants people to exercise. Kept hounding me to do it with him until I flatly told him to forget it."

John chuckled. "I suppose he would have proposed if you'd been willing."

She stood up. "How do you know he didn't propose anyway? I am loveable, you know."

He reached for her and pulled her into his arms. "Do I know that! Let's go to bed."

She laughed and pulled away. "Not now. Don't we have to save Alex from a fate worse than death? I know what your problem is. You're jealous. You wish you had someone age 30 to marry."

He pulled her back into his embrace. "No, darling. Since I met you I've wanted no one but you and you know it. I've asked you to marry me a hundred times. You always say no and, I try to understand, but I can't really see why."

He took her face between his hands. "Since Alex is marrying, at 90, surely you won't think it obscene for two old people like us."

Indignantly she pulled away, "I've never thought it obscene." Then added, "And don't say we're old."

"Liz, for God's sake. Why do you hate that word? It's just a word. It won't bite."

She said thoughtfully, "No. It won't bite."

Tears came unbidden. "If it bit me I could swat it like a mosquito and get rid of it."

John couldn't help but wince at the haunted look in her eyes.

She shook her head. "No, John. It doesn't bite. It corrodes. Every time I hear it, when it's referring to me, a little piece of me flakes away, like bits of rust."

She stopped for a moment and took a deep breath. "How many bits do I have left? I try to ignore it. I pretend it doesn't matter. I even convince myself sometimes, but only the other day I was astounded when someone told me I was almost 80."

She shuddered. "The possibility I could be that old, was a horror I had with me for days. I think of myself as still the young woman I used to be. I play at being gay and giddy. Most people see me that way, including you, but that word old eats at me like a cancer. That's why I've begged you not to use it."

"I had no idea," John said. "I know your age and it has never bothered me. I would still love to have you as my wife. Or just move in with me. I would love to have you with me all the time."

"No, John. I love you very much but I also love my time alone, as you do. Admit it. You don't want anyone else around when you're writing. I'm the same way, and if I'm not writing, I still like the solitude."

"But there are times I really need you."

"Yes, I know, and there are times when I need you, but not all the time. If we were married I'd feel I was letting you down if I wasn't by your side at all times."

"But that's where I want you to be."

"No you don't. Think of the circuits you make, to talk- shows and things like that. You wouldn't feel you could flirt with the women. If you did flirt, you'd feel unfaithful. No. I don't want that for either of us."

He pushed her away and looked into her eyes. "You mean if we were married I could no longer flirt? My God, I had no idea. That would be terrible."

He stepped back, grinned at her and said with glee. "I knew there was a reason Alex shouldn't marry. I'll tell him what he'll be missing. It'll stop him in his tracks."

He gave her another hug and said, "We'd better get ready. We're to meet Alex and his fiancée at Ginnys restaurant."

"I don't think I've ever been there," she said. "I suppose it's posh."

"Actually it's not posh. People go there in blue jeans and cut offs. It just happens to be the 'in' place at this time and you know Alex. He wants to be where the action is."

"I don't have any blue jeans but I don't want to meet his fiancée looking tacky. I'll get dressed."

When they arrived at the restaurant, it seemed others had also wanted to dress. There wasn't a blue jean to be seen.

As they approached Alex's table he rose to greet them. Annaliz had a good look at the woman with him. Dear God. She can't be a day younger than 70. Her neck is as scrawny as mine.

She took another look and thought, what a beautiful dress, it must have been designed by an international fashion designer. It was a plain sheath, made so well it fit the curves of her body. The fabric was India silk, shimmering in the soft, restaurant light.

Alex introduced Esperanza with pride and Annaliz could see why the woman had impressed him. She had poise, a model's way of holding herself, and she had a ready smile, all things Annaliz liked in a woman.

"I'm glad to meet you at last," Esperanza said. "Alex has told me so much about you both."

She looked at John. "You're astounded I'm not 30 years old. As you can see, I am of an age."

With true gallantry John said, "You are ageless. No wonder Alex fell for you."

"Esperanza." Alex said. "I need to watch out for this man. If I'm not careful he'll take you away from me."

"I don't think so," she said. "Look at the way he looks at Annaliz. He wouldn't be interested in me."

John nodded. "I am one of Annaliz' followers. She is a wonderful woman and many men have been after her."

Annaliz laughed. "You said the magic words, 'have been.' I sit back now and admire women like you, Esperanza, so disgustingly beautiful and young."

She grinned at her. "Don't give in to the sweet words these fellows are plying us with. It's the same old line."

"No. No," Alex exclaimed. "I am in love, truly in love, for the first time in a hundred years."

Esperanza looked at him with a frown. "One hundred years? You told me you were only 90."

The laughter that ensued, paved the way to an enjoyable evening. When the women were in the rest room together, Annaliz asked Esperanza where she got the beautiful dress she was wearing.

"I designed it myself." She said. "Didn't Alex tell you I have been a fashion designer for many years in Mexico City?"

"I haven't seen him for the past three months. I believe he must have been in the City, courting you."

"Yes. I have held off on a promise of marriage. I have been there four times already. I wasn't sure I wanted to do it again, but Alex is very persuasive."

She went on, "He keeps telling me he's rich, as if that would sway me. I have been very successful in my business and do not need his money."

"If you design dresses like this one I can see why you are successful."

She wanted to confide in this woman and tell her about Tiffany but knew this was not the time or place. This was a night for celebration, not for sorrow.

Back in the hotel, cuddled close beside John in their bed, Annaliz said, "Alex is lucky. I think he has found a woman who can keep up with him, step by step. She is fabulous. Didn't you think so?"

"I didn't pay much attention, love. I kept looking at you. You become more beautiful every year."

Paying no attention to the complement she said, "You know, John. I almost told her about Tiffany but I was afraid I would break down if I did and I didn't want to do it in front of someone I had just met."

"Tiffany is constantly in your thoughts, isn't she?"

"Yes. She would have been so happy to see the dress Esperanza wore. To be on the verge of becoming famous herself, then being struck down by cancer. It doesn't seem fair."

"My love, you know the world is not fair."

"But why was it necessary to remove a breast, when having a gorgeous figure helped get her this far in the design world? She was her own best model." Annaliz began to weep.

John held her closer. "Go ahead and cry, honey. I didn't think you had any tears left, but I see you do. I can remember when Jorge died, I didn't think you would ever stop crying."

"To lose someone I loved so much without being able to say goodbye; it was devastating. Thank God I had you. You were there, understanding my need. I can never thank you enough."

Changing the subject, John said, "You told me Tiffany was weathering this operation well."

"Oh, she is. After it was over, she joked she now had a new field for her design work. She would make a dress, not for the woman who had everything but for the one who 'did not' have everything. She meant it to be funny but I cried. How could my daughter be so brave?"

"She takes after her mother, I guess. You have always been tough."

"Tiffany was the sensitive one in the family. She felt things more than anyone else. I know this has been rough on her but she's not going to give up or give in. She's fighting now to get Henry off her back. He's begging her to take him back. He keeps telling her she needs him now since she's 'disabled'. How she hates that label."

She said angrily, "I always knew I disliked Henry. There were times, when I was visiting her, I could have killed him."

"Come, darling. Don't get any more upset. I'll hold you until you fall asleep."

20

Alex and Esperanza decided to get married in the old house in August. The restoration would be complete.

He reminded Annaliz of her wish to put fresh flowers in every room. She said, "I plan to make the house look like a florist's shop."

He told her he was inviting only special people to the wedding and since he wanted to use the huge dining room table they had found on the first day, he had limited his invitations to 10 people.

"You and John will be two of the honored guests." Alex said.

"We definitely will be honored," Annaliz said.

She knew the wedding would probably include the mayor of Mazatlan, the governor of Sinaloa, and probably someone in politics in Mexico City. Alex was well known for his behind-the-scenes maneuvering when politicians needed to get re-elected.

"There will be a reception later," he said. "It will be in the ball room. I'll invite the whole neighborhood to that."

He probably will too, Annaliz thought. I wouldn't be surprised to find the maids, gardeners, their spouses and children at the affair. Alex is one friendly guy.

The feast, catered by the Playa, was magnificent. Annaliz liked the way she had arranged roses on the table. They were laid in profusion down the center, enabling everyone to talk across the table without being hindered by bowls of flowers.

The table was large enough to have huge platters placed on each side of the flowers. These were filled with chicken and what looked like a whole pig. There was roast beef, and of course shrimp. Shrimp came in cocktails, in white wine sauce, in the salad. After all, wasn't Mazatlan the shrimp capitol of the world?

The dishes Annaliz liked best at any fancy table were the fruit plates. There was one piled so high she gasped to see the way it was arranged. There was watermelon on the bottom, making a beautiful contrast with the color of the bananas, which made up the next layer; then red papaya, showing the green guava on top of it to perfection.

She knew Mexicans loved maraschino cherries, so was not surprised to see a mound of them on the very top, with the stems standing upright, waiting for the first person to take one or two.

True to Mexican tradition, the first person to be served was the host, Alex, looking very Spanish in his white, ruffled shirt, black pants and a black jacket, embroidered in red.

The bride was not in wedding white, but dressed in a shimmering red dress, with the full skirt of the Spanish dancer. Her hair, dressed high on top of her head, had a wisp or two out of place.

Annaliz knew full well the hairdresser had planned for this to happen. Esperanza was not the type to have hair fall where she did not want it to fall.

When everyone rose, after dinner, she was surprised to see Esperanza was wearing high-heeled boots.

A local band in the ballroom, played the old Mexican favorites. Annaliz was amazed to see her grandson, Peter, with his new girl friend, doing the tango.

I didn't realize the whole family had been invited.

Karen was sitting off to one side with other women, as though dancing was not meant for her group.

I should have known, Annaliz thought. There goes Tiffany dancing with Pedro, Estrella's husband. She seems to always find the best-looking man in the crowd.

All around her, people of all ages were dancing; men and women and papas with their children. It was delightful to watch.

Every one was dressed in the best they had. The little girl's clothing, probably their communion dresses, were so white it almost hurt one's eyes.

Annaliz insisted that she and John dance the first two dances. They then circled the room, talking to old friends. It seemed Alex knew and had invited everyone in town.

Suddenly the music changed to the familiar flamenco sound, and the guests, knowing what was to come, began moving back against the walls, to clear a space in the middle of the huge room.

A woman appeared first, dressed in red, her high-heeled boots tapping out a challenge.

"Aaah." The sound went around the room as, one by one, they realized it was the bride, dancing the traditional Spanish dance.

Esperanza was a beautiful dancer, swinging her full skirts in time with the music, tapping a rhythm with her boots; actually tapping out a challenge; daring anyone to come and dance with her.

Alex came through a side door, tapping as he came, arms held stiffly behind his back, wearing a huge Mexican sombrero.

Annaliz wanted to clap but knew it was not appropriate at this time. Tears came instead. This was a dance of love.

The two dancers had eyes only for one another. The challenge was there, then the giving in, then the challenge again.

Without thinking, Annaliz' put out her hand to find John's and found his searching for hers.

In a whisper he said, "You're feeling it too?"

"Oh, yes. I can see this same fiesta in this house two hundred years ago. It's

313

as though we're there, in that time, watching a bride and groom celebrate their wedding. I shall never forget this moment."

21

Alex and Esperanza left for their month long honeymoon. John had gone to Chicago to give a lecture and Annaliz was seated in her patio, trying not to think of the letter which had arrived that morning from Tiffany.

"The doctors have found a lump in my other breast and are going to do a biopsy. They say it probably isn't cancer but they want to be sure.

No. I don't want you to come. You hover and I don't want it. I remember you never liked it either so I'm sure you'll understand. Karen is bad enough.

Pray for me, Mom. I thought I was adjusted, as well as one could be, but I find this difficult to take. The operation is on the 14th. I'll let you know as soon as I get the results."

Annaliz had placed the letter upside down on the hall table. She didn't even want to look at it. There was nothing she could do but wait it out. She wanted to be there, to hold Tiffany in her arms and tell her it would get better. She knew it might not. It might get worse. I do wish there was something I could do to help her. She looked around the patio, the place she thought the most tranquil in the world, and wished Tiffany could be with her right now, instead of waiting and wondering what the results of the biopsy would be. With difficulty, Annaliz got down on her knees. She had not been there for a long time but felt it meant more, somehow, to do something as important as this, correctly.

"Dear God," she prayed. "I've been thanking You all these years for the blessings You've showered on me, but now I..." She wept hot tears and sobbed before she could continue. "Now, I'm asking You to take my blessings and use them to help Tiffany get through this ordeal. I'm an old woman." She wiped her eyes and added, "and You know I don't say that to just anyone, but I am, and I'll gladly give up my remaining years, if You'll let me take on whatever is eating at Tiffany. Send it to me, Lord. Give her a chance to have the wonderful life she has planned for herself, and thank You for listening to me."

She had to pull herself up by hanging on to a branch of the Jacaranda tree. Once again seated she thought, God has answered my prayers over the years. Maybe not as I would always want them to be answered, but my life has turned out well. I want something as good for Tiffany.

Annaliz didn't think she would make it through the week, which seemed to last forever, but finally Karen called and said the lump in Tiffany's breast was benign. "I thought surely you'd come for this operation. It might have been worse, you know. You should have been here."

"She asked me not to come. She didn't want me and she's wise enough to make her own decisions."

"You should have been here, anyway. Mothers are supposed to be there when their children are going through something like this, no matter how old the child is."

"Tiffany doesn't like hovering any more than I do," Annaliz said. "For Heaven's sake, give her some space to live her own life. She needs to be alone for awhile to decide what she will do next."

"Oh, I know what she's doing next. She's going to Chicago to a fashion show. She's going to parade what she calls her 'fall line'."

"You sound as though you're objecting. I think it would be good for her. She would be busy. She wouldn't have time to think about her health."

"That's just it. Neither of us is getting any younger. Age does take a lot out of you…"

Annaliz couldn't keep from interrupting. "Karen, when you get a lot older you'll look back on this conversation and laugh. When you are 75 or 80 you'll wonder what people are thinking of when they speak of age. You'll find life can be just as exciting and invigorating as it was at 30 or 40. Maybe even more. You won't think of your years but only how you can enjoy them."

"Well, maybe if we were like you, Mom. You've never had a sick day in your life, so it's easy to say one shouldn't worry about falling ill. I know, from experience, illnesses do come when you least expect them. One of these days it will happen to you. Just you wait and see."

Annaliz hung up, thinking of the time she'd had hepatitis. She was in the hospital for three weeks but the doctors had convinced her she wasn't going to die from it so she never told the family. Why worry them un-necessarily? She had recovered from strep throat one winter and knew she had been lucky it wasn't any worse. Again she had found an excuse not to let the family know. They would have come, then would have insisted she go back to the States for treatment. No, she thought, As far as they know I've never had a sick day in my life and I want them to go on thinking that way.

Tiffany insisted her mother be at her fall showing, even when Annaliz used the cliché, "I have nothing to wear to such a fashionable occasion."

"I'm taking care of it," Tiffany said, "I've fashioned a new dress for you. You're going to love it, Mom."

"Don't give me any of those slinky things, honey. You know I don't have the figure for it. No matter how I try, things keep sagging."

"I promise it's not like that," She said. "I've designed something for Karen too. I'm sure she'll be thrilled, and hers isn't slinky. She doesn't have the figure for it either."

"Heavens! I hope you haven't told her."

"Mom, I'm not stupid. Come on. You'll love Chicago."

She giggled. "John is there, you know. He's lecturing at one of the Universities."

"Yes, I know. Why are you laughing?"

"I can't help it, Mom. I know Alex got married at 90 and I didn't laugh then. I thought it was lovely."

She giggled again. "It's just - you're my Mom. Moms aren't supposed to go to bed with anyone."

Annaliz said, "If moms didn't go to bed with anyone, you wouldn't be here. Get used to it, honey. I'll live my life the way I want to. I don't want any laughter from you, do you hear?"

Karen had large hips and Tiffany had designed an A- frame skirt, very simple. One noticed the skirt and not the hips and Karen paraded back and forth and kept asking her mother if the dress was too young for her.

Annaliz' dress was a tent. That's what she called it. It had a huge ruffled collar, similar to the kind worn by Queen Elizabeth, and the rest of the green dress fell in tiny pleats from the shoulder to the floor. Monk's sleeves, wide from the shoulder to the wrist, enabled Annaliz to hide her hands if she wished to. She said it felt like a caftan but had much more style.

What she had not realized was her dress and Karen's were to be part of the fashion show.

"No way am I going to walk down a ramp," she said, "I know my limitations and that's one of them." She moved around the room, holding up the hem of the dress she was wearing, showing a bit of leg. "Can't you just see me?" She walked back and forth, swinging her hips, mincing along as though she were wearing high heels. "Can't you hear the laughter and the cat-calls?"

Her walk slowed and she said, "I'd probably lose my balance and fall down, right in the middle of the runway. The onlookers would laugh, and rightly so. I can hear them say, 'Look at the old woman, trying to be a model.' I won't do it and that's final. I'll make other plans."

Tiffany howled with laughter. "Mom, I'm not asking you to walk down the ramp. I want Karen to walk with the other models. I want you to be present for the afternoon tea I'm giving for the buyers. I want you to walk around, looking as regal as I know you can, and let everyone ask who you are and who designed that dress."

She went on, "When they know you're a well-known poet they'll fall over themselves to be introduced. You'll have an opportunity to tell them I designed it especially for you."

"I'm not well-known any more, Tiffany. That was over ten years ago." She grinned. "And this sounds like crass salesmanship to me."

"I don't care what it's called, Mom. It sells clothes. I've seen other designers do the same thing and the buyers flock in. They like the free champagne, I guess. You will come to the tea, won't you?"

"Of course I will. I'll make sure to be the hit of the afternoon."

This turned out to be true as two different buyers, whose firms catered to large women, liked the idea of being able to show a dress that had no size. They were sure it would be a hit. As one said, "One-size-fits-all appeals to these ladies. Then they don't have to let the world know they wear a size XXL."

John and Annaliz spent only one day together because he had to get to New York for a conference. They went to the University, where he had given a speech the night before, and talked to some of the students.

It was a new experience for Annaliz and she enjoyed the young people, who seemed to be interested in her life as well as John's. Some of them knew her poetry and asked her to recite. She stood up and spoke with no notes. Afterward she wondered how she could have remembered something she had written over ten years before. Maybe it's because it's Jorge's poetry. I wrote it when he was with me. It's still there in my heart, I guess.

The fashion show was a success for Tiffany. She wanted to get home to start work on her next collection and Karen flew with Annaliz to Mazatlan for a short vacation.

Karen came out of the house at eleven the next morning. "Look at you." She said to Annaliz, "Every time I come, you're sitting in that chair. Does anything ever happen around here?"

"Why, yes." Annaliz answered. "Just this morning a new hatch of yellow butterflies covered the hedge."

"What's so great about butterflies?"

"Well, I knew they were a gift from God, sent especially to brighten my day."

"Oh, Mom. You talk about God as though you know Him personally."

"I do know Him personally. It's the only way anyone knows Him."

"I mean, you're not religious. You don't even go to church."

"Don't you believe, Karen?"

"Sure I do. I go to church every Sunday."

"That's not what I asked."

"I'm a lot more religious than you. I sent my kids to church, which was more than you did, and I see that my grandchildren go to Sunday School. Do I believe? Of course I believe. I'm very religious."

Knowing this conversation was going nowhere, Annaliz suggested they go to lunch, which meant to Karen something was happening and she was happy.

When in bed that night, Annaliz said, "Thank You, God, for helping me keep my temper this morning. Karen is so positive about everything there are times I'd like to smack her but I know You wouldn't approve. Thank You for sending the butterflies. They made the hedge look as though it were gold-plated. I liked that touch."

Karen must have felt better the next day. She planned an outing for them to spend a few days in Guadalajara, then she wanted to see the weavers in Ajijic everyone raved about. Arriving in Ajijic in the evening, they took a room at the Posada. Annaliz was delighted to be entertained at dinner with a local trio, who were celebrating the fact their new CD was a best seller.

Then it was on to Tlaquepaque to watch the glass blowers and the metal-working artisans at work. They had lunch at the restaurant with no name, enjoying the garden environment and the peacocks strolling through it.

It took a week of their time and Annaliz knew Karen had gone home happy. She thinks that in the last few days she's filled her mother's life with things she wouldn't do for herself.

I'm sure she's happy that she had the chance to show me there is more to life than just sitting in a chair in the patio. She will keep on believing, as I know she does, that a few butterflies on the hedge won't mean a thing to someone who has now seen more of the world.

She doesn't realize butterflies mean more to me than material things like woven cloth and glass bottles. It was good to spend a few days with her, doing what she enjoys, but I still prefer sitting in my chair in the patio.

22

It had been one of those wonderful sunny afternoons in Mazatlan. Sitting in her favorite chair in the patio, wondering idly what to have for dinner, Annaliz was startled when Tiffany came running through the house.

"Mom, I have to talk to you."

"You made me jump." Annaliz said. "I didn't know you were coming. Why didn't you call?"

Tiffany said, "I hadn't planned to come. I've been in California, visiting Dad. He's dying, Mom. He wants you to come see him."

She looked at her daughter with a frown. "I have nothing to say to your dad, my dear. I said it all a long time ago."

"I know you've hated him since the divorce but he's dying and it seems the compassionate thing to do to grant his last wish."

"I've never hated anyone in my life, but I have to admit I came close to it with him. I don't want to see him."

"He's my father, Mom. Can't you do this for me?"

"Did he say what he wanted to talk to me about?"

"Well, he didn't spell it out but it sounds as though he wants you to forgive him. He's evidently sorry now for the way he treated you."

Annaliz snorted. "He's making his peace with God, is he?"

"Mom, how can you be so mean? That's not like you. The man is dying."

"Tiffany, this is the first time in many years you've even mentioned your father. I didn't know you ever saw him. Did he call and ask you to go see him?"

"Yes. It's true I haven't seen him in many years but he is my father. His wife died several years ago and he says he has been all alone and lonely."

Annaliz asked, "Did he ask you to bring Karen with you to see him?"

"No. He asked me to come by myself. I don't know why."

"Oh, I know why. He knows you're the sensitive one in the family. He wants sympathy. He knows you kids well enough to know Karen would probably bawl him out for not keeping in touch with the family."

Annaliz looked at her daughter and asked, "Did you tell Karen you were going?"

"No, Mom, he asked me not to."

"That should have told you something. You'd think, if he was on his deathbed, he would want to see both his children."

She shook her head and sighed, "Tiffany. He's up to his old tricks. He wants someone to feel sorry for him. He isn't thinking of you and your feelings.

He's only concerned with himself. He hasn't changed a bit."

"You haven't seen him, Mom. You wouldn't recognize him. He's just skin and bones and his hair has fallen out. He has cancer of the colon. He says they didn't catch it early enough and now he's dying."

"Sounds just like him," Annaliz said. "Now he's blaming the doctors for not catching his cancer in time."

Tiffany turned away, tears in her eyes. "I know you never loved him, but couldn't you, just this once, quit thinking of yourself and do what he asks?"

Horrified that Tiffany, of all people, thought her incapable of thinking of anyone but herself, Annaliz said, "So. It has come to this. After all these years, he is finally turning my children against me."

"I'm not against you," Tiffany cried. "I just want everyone to be happy. It's such a small thing to ask. One day out of your life, to make someone else's last minutes more pleasurable, doesn't seem like much to ask."

"It may not seem like much to you, Tiffany, but I value every one of my days. I do not want to spend what could be my last one, talking to Darrell, no matter how ill he is."

"How can I tell him that? It sounds so uncaring."

"You can tell him anything you want. If he has a message for me he can give it to you and you can tell me. I know what it would be like if I went. He might start out saying he was sorry but before the visit was over he would tell me all the things that went wrong in our marriage were my fault. I'm sorry, honey, but I refuse to listen to another of his tirades."

Tiffany decided to return to her father that afternoon. "He might be dying while I'm standing here, Mom. I wish you would come with me but if you won't I still have to go to him. He needs someone."

Annaliz thought, I was enjoying this day until she came. I have tried, over the years, to put all thought of Darrell out of my mind. After my divorce, whenever I would unconsciously think of something that had caused me anguish during my marriage, I would say to myself: "Don't go down that road. That way be dragons."

Now the dragons have found me. Am I a mean person, as Tiffany said? Annaliz spent a sleepless night, wondering if she had been mean, or if she had made the right decision.

When I first met Darrell, she thought the next morning, I was so enchanted with his easy smile and loving ways, I was sure I had found the man for me. I had no idea, until we had been married about a month, that this man was a sadist. He seemed to get pleasure from making other people miserable. The simplest little thing would set him off. If I didn't have dinner on the table on time he would go into a rage. He screamed at me and at the children. If there was a toy left out, instead of being in the toy box, he would be so sarcastic to the children they would cry. Some nights he'd say, "How could I have picked such a stupid woman? Can't even control your own kids. I come home to the mess they've made and you haven't done a damn thing about it. I'm going out to eat. You make me sick."

Not only the children would cry. I would too. I can't believe Tiffany doesn't remember how afraid she was of him. She used to run to her room and sob for hours.

She is kind-hearted. She believes the best of everyone. I know this is hard for her. She's had cancer, so she knows what a difficult time it can be for anyone, and she wants to make his passing as easy as possible.

He knew she would be compassionate, so he called her. Now he's dying, he wants someone to hold his hand. It's a pity he didn't give that kind of consideration to others before this happened. Perhaps, then, they would be more willing to help him.

When John came that evening, she told him of her daughter's visit. His reaction was similar to Tiffany's. "You could have gone," he said. "It would only take a day or two. The poor guy must be really suffering."

"I can't believe this," Annaliz said. "I thought I told you how Darrell treated me in our marriage. Why would I want to go? Just to listen to another screaming fit? No thanks."

"I didn't think you hated him so much," John said.

"You sound just like Tiffany. I don't hate him. I just don't want to have any dealings with him. I went through years of trying to make him love me. Instead I was beat down until there was no me left. I won't go through that again and I don't think you have the right to tell me I should."

"I am sorry," he said. "I didn't know you felt so strongly about it. Of course, you shouldn't go." He reached over and patted her hand. "You must have loved him once."

"I don't want to talk about it," she said. "What was your day like? Better than mine, I hope."

"Well," he said slowly, "Let's see. I spent the day wishing I were with my favorite girl. I kept thinking how long the day was until dinnertime, when I would be with her."

"Oh, John. I've been beside myself today. I haven't made dinner."

She stomped her foot. "It makes me mad to think Darrell can upset me this much, after so many years."

"Dinner isn't important," he said. "I just love being with you. How about if I make waffles? You know I can make waffles."

She looked at him and smiled for the first time that day. "Yes, you can make waffles." Trying to laugh, she said,

337

"You can make them at your house because you have a waffle iron. I do not have one, so no matter how good you are at making them, you can't do it here."

"Damn, woman. You know I like to make them. Why don't you buy an iron?"

"And have no excuse to go to your house. No way."

He chuckled. "Aha. You like going to my house. Why don't you come stay there with me? We could have waffles every morning."

"No thanks," she said. "In a few weeks we'd be tired of both waffles and each other."

She looked around the kitchen. "It looks like we'll have to have peanut butter sandwiches. Do you like yours with jelly or without?"

"I don't care for it either way," he said. "We need some cheering up, and we sure can't do it with peanut butter. Why don't we go to Casa Country and enjoy the floor show? Their dancing waiters always make you laugh."

As they got in the car, Annaliz thought, Thank you, God, for giving me John in my later years. I need someone sensible and loving right now.

They drove along the sea-wall road and she could see the surf, white against the sand, and was reminded of her first view of this beautiful spot. I was running from my husband and my critics. Then I felt I was in Heaven where no one could touch me. I was sure I would never have to listen to sarcasm again. Yet here in Mazatlan, years later, even if I don't want him to be, Darrell is in my thoughts.

I'm sure, when people at home hear I refused to go to his dying bedside, the talk will begin again. I can just hear them: "She was always the selfish one, only thinking of herself."

Why do people we know, especially family, try to send us on guilt trip after guilt trip? I don't believe in guilt and refuse to accept it. And I definitely will not change my mind about going to see Darrell but there is a nagging little voice in the back of my mind that keeps whispering, "You could have gone. It wouldn't have killed you."

23

Alex called ship to shore, to tell John he and Esperanza would be arriving in Mazatlan on the 30th of September. The cruise ship they had been on, for their honeymoon, was coming in that night at nine o'clock and would dock the next day.

"We can take a launch from the ship to the pier. Could you meet us?" he asked.

"Hey," John said. "It's Annaliz' birthday. I was hoping to take her somewhere special. It would be nice if we could have dinner together. She'd like that, I know."

"If it's her birthday why don't we have dinner here on the ship? The chef is fabulous and the Captain is a charmer. I'll ask him if he can dine with us in his uniform. That always seems to please the ladies."

A few minutes later, Alex called back. "Esperanza wants to know why we can't make it a surprise birthday party for Annaliz and invite her family and friends?"

"You don't surprise her very often." John said. "She says she hates surprises. If we invited the family she'd find out and wiggle out of it somehow."

"We won't tell her we've invited the family. I think they ought to be here on her birthday. Why aren't they doing something for her?"

"Karen told me they only do a birthday party every five years after the age of 70."

"That's ridiculous," Alex said. "What if someone died before the next party? Think how horrible they'd feel."

"Well, I'd feel that, but I'm not sure her family would. They are so set in doing things as they have always done them, I'm not sure they'd show up for this if you invited them."

"Don't worry," Alex said. "I have yet to know a woman who would turn down a chance to dine with the captain of a ship. I'll talk to them. They'll come."

John called Annaliz. "Hi darling. Alex called from the cruise ship. They're coming in the night of your birthday and when I told him, he said they always had a captain's dinner the last night out and he would like us to dine with them. Is it okay with you?"

"Of course, but please tell him not to make a big thing out of my birthday. I don't want any special attention."

"Don't worry. I'll tell Alex to tone it down. I was going to take you to Salvadore's, the new restaurant in town, but this sounds like more fun."

He hesitated, then said, "Your family aren't planning anything are they?"

"Heaven's no. They give birthday parties for me only every five years. I still have a year to go."

When talking to Tiffany a few days later, Annaliz mentioned she and John were having dinner on the cruise ship. "Since I've never been on a cruise it should be interesting to see how the other half lives." She added, "We've been invited to join the passengers for a last dinner before the ship docks."

"You mean you're dining with the captain?"

"That's what John said. You sound as though it's something special."

"But it is, Mom. Most women on cruises never get to dine with the captain. Of course, Alex would have no problem. I'm sure the crew were falling over themselves to do whatever he or Esperanza wanted while they were on board."

"You mean because he's such a big tipper?"

"Partly, but mainly because he's so charming no one could resist him."

"Well, we'll see," Annaliz said. "I'll tell you all about it afterward."

Tiffany asked. "What are you going to wear?"

"If it's so fancy I suppose I should wear the tent you made me. You said I looked regal in that. I'll charm the captain for sure."

Sounding insulted but laughing, Tiffany said, "It is not a tent. It is my Elizabeth gown worn by the best of women."

"By the biggest, you mean. I love it, my dear. I really do. I'm always happy to be seen in it."

"I'm sure you'll be the belle of the ball," Tiffany said.

Getting ready to go meet the captain, Annaliz looked at herself in the mirror, for the first time in a long time, and had to admit there was a certain something about the dress that made her look like a queen.

Yes, she thought, the wrinkles are still there but the soft green of the dress softens them. I'll smile a lot. I notice, when I do, the wrinkles just sort of disappear and this dress is wonderful in another way. It hides my scrawny neck.

The only way I can hide it normally, is by wearing turtle-necks. Funny. I didn't used to like them much, but in the last few years they have become a necessity.

Will I be regal enough for the big shot, she wondered? Should I shove my bangs back up a bit, as Karen is always telling me to do? Should I wear more blush? Oh, heck, if I'm not what the captain is expecting, I guess he can have me thrown overboard.

John picked her up in a white limousine. When she protested, he said, "Your dress deserves to be in a limo, not in my dirty old car."

"Oh," she said. "It's not me but the dress you're enamored with."

He grinned. "Of course. I thought you knew. I have a thing about women's clothes, especially one's worn by beautiful women."

"I wish you wouldn't say I'm beautiful, John. I know better, and it's lovely to hear, but it also embarrasses me when you do it front of other people."

"My love," he said. "You're beautiful to me. You grow lovelier every year. Please don't deprive me of the chance to pay a compliment."

"What about those wrinkles you refer to now and then? They certainly are not beautiful, so how can you tell such lies?" She grinned. "It isn't because I don't like to hear them, but please don't do it in front of anyone else."

"I only say that about your face when you make me mad. You know I love every wrinkle you have. Sometimes I say you have too many but you know I don't mean it."

"When I look in the mirror I know how correct you are."

"Quit looking then and just believe me."

At the dock, several sailors dressed in white escorted them to a launch. Seated in the stern of the craft, watching the spray form a rooster tail, was exhilarating. Maybe I should take a cruise, she thought. This is fun.

The launch took them out into the bay to the cruise ship. When they reached it, they were escorted up the ramp to the dining room. Annaliz was amazed. The huge room was resplendent with many small tables, covered in white linen. Large bouquets of flowers, in tall vases, stood in front of a bandstand.

The buffet table, laden with enough food to feed an army, had a large ice sculpture in the center. It looks like Queen Elizabeth, she thought. Oh, no. Alex knew I loved this dress and he had the cook do this to celebrate my birthday.

Darn him. I wish he wasn't so eager to celebrate anything and everything.

She could see why women were pleased to be invited to the captain's table. He had many medals on the front of his uniform. He's really dressed up, Annaliz thought. He came to her, saluted, and said, "At your service, Madam."

She gave a small curtsy and smiled at him. He presented his arm and led her to a table in the center. When she and John were seated a band began to play. I knew it, she said to herself. It's 60's music. Alex has even told the band it's my birthday.

She was hungry and wondered when they were supposed to eat. The buffet looked awfully good. She could see the waiters putting finishing touches to the table. The lovely odor of roast beef filled the room.

The dining room had begun to fill with people of all ages. These must be the guests of the ship, eating their last meal before they dock. They look very festive. Everyone seems to be dressed up, as if for a party. I guess the last night out must be as important as Tiffany said.

The captain came back to their table. "Would you mind?" he asked. "The band leader would like to meet you. It seems he loves your poetry and would like you to autograph a book for him."

She thought this was a strange request, at such a time, but she went with him, up a couple of steps to the bandstand. As she started to reach out a hand, to greet a man with a guitar, the captain turned her around and announced, "Ladies and Gentlemen. Please make welcome, Annaliz, the birthday girl."

The clapping began and Annaliz hated Alex at that moment. She didn't know these people. How could he have thought she would enjoy being paraded...

She gasped. Out of a side door came Ramona, Lorena, Esperanza, Alex,

Estrella, Karen, Tiffany and several grandchildren. Behind them came a waiter bearing a huge birthday cake.

John came to help her down from the stand and she whispered to him. "There's been a terrible mistake. This is not the right year. I'm only 79."

John laughed with pleasure. "You are surprised then? It was Esperanza's idea."

"How did she get the family to come? They don't believe in celebrating every year."

John laughed. "Maybe it was the fact they would dine with a captain that brought them. See? She planned it so they would sit at his table. Even Karen is impressed."

Dinner was over and after dancing two dances with John and several with her grandchildren, Annaliz sat, watching the others having fun.

John looks tired. It has been a long night. The captain and crew have really outdone themselves. I don't think I've ever had a better time.

It's amazing the way Alex got everyone to participate. I didn't think the family would budge out of their rut to come to Mazatlan, on an off year, just for my birthday, but it was awfully nice having them.

Glancing down at her feet she thought, these damn shoes Tiffany insists I wear with this dress are killing me and my knee is giving me fits.

She sighed. Maybe I just don't like to admit I'm exhausted. Is it possible I might be getting too old for these festivities? She caught herself up short. For Heaven's sake, what am I saying? Of course I'm not too old. I'll never be that old. I intend to go on until I drop.

She reached her hand across the table, "John, my dear, are you too tired for one more dance?"

She stood up and suddenly began to feel the old familiar tingle in her legs, the fullness in her head. Oh, dear God, not here, not now. She turned a terrified face to John.

He took one look at her and pulled her into his arms. "Darling, what is it? What's wrong?"

She began to sag toward the floor. It was all he could do to hold her. Peter saw what was happening and ran to help. They carried her to a couch in the lounge and sent for a doctor.

After a few minutes she opened her eyes, looked up at Karen, hovering above her, and said slowly, "I suppose now you'll…"

She sighed. Her eyes closed again and, so low they had trouble hearing her, she murmured, "I had made other plans."

Printed in the United States
15937LVS00001B/13-21